To Elinor – still with the
American Red Cross is
stationed at the United States
Naval Hospital – Astoria Oregon.
A Merry Christmas
Mother + Dad –

December 25 – 1945

BEACH RED

BEACH RED

A NOVEL BY

PETER BOWMAN

RANDOM HOUSE · NEW YORK

TO THE UNRETURNING

BEACH RED

Oh, say, can you see by the dawn's early light
the glimmering haze squatting on its moist gray haunches and
guarding the waters with a battleship resting across its knees,
searching in diminishing circles until it challenges its own eyes?

The transport heaves at anchor and you sit on deck
with your combat pack harnessed, your rifle cleaned and ready
and your steel helmet claiming identity with those surrounding you—
assigned to its proper cluster in a field of mushrooms.

The stars that had pinned up the curtain of darkness
are beginning to loosen and fall spinning into the sea,
and there are sucking waves and there are creaking hawsers
and the smell of sweat and gun oil and leather
and clothes in which men have tried to capture sleep.

You lounge with intense casualness, waiting for the company commander
to emerge from the wardroom where lights burned all night
and low voices had planned and exhorted and said Amen.

It's all finished now; the briefing, the study of maps,
the review of reconnaissance reports from the various landing beaches,
the forecasts as to the probable condition of the surf,
the distribution of airphotos showing high and low tide views,
the marking of passages and points navigable by small craft,
the calculation of wind direction for laying down smoke screens,
the division into boat groups, the arrangement of assault schedules,
the elaborate checking and tabulation of supply and control facilities
and the selection of suitable assembly points in forward areas.

Unit meetings were held and innumerable small conferences took place.
Excitement transmitted itself from man to man in little shocks
and all during the early hours rumors were snatched at
and fierce arguments over nothing in particular rose and subsided.
Then came the last quiet waiting, and chill, fluttering wisps
of hushed tension smothered your gaping senses. This is it . . .

Now the door opens and Captain MacDonald spills the light
and dams it up quickly and steps to the deck.
He peers at his wrist and says, "All right, men,
twenty-five seconds to hell!" Then he gives a redheaded grin
and plucks the twin silver bars from his junglesuited shoulders,
stuffing them in a pocket. "Listen, fellows—from now on
just call me Mac. And I'll court martial any guy
who throws me a salute when the Japs are looking."

His arm lifts. "Twenty!" . . . Time was inducted into the Army,
relinquishing, as a matter of course, its nonessential civilian occupation.
It was processed at the reception center of duration plus,
examined as to elapsing periods or temporal defects of posteriority
and outfitted with G.I. clothing and equipment in chronological order.

"Fifteen!" . . . Time was insured into perpetuity against its ultimate stoppage,
housed and cared for in continuity at per diem rates
and fed a scientifically balanced diet of years and months
with weeks, days, hours and minutes served as supplementary nutrients
on the understanding that seconds were readily obtainable on request.

"Ten!" . . . Time trained in accordance with War Department circular 187
which states that after any similarity it may have had
to its past, present or future is rendered purely coincidental,
it shall be promoted in rank and authorized to wear
the uniform recognized as denoting 24 hours instead of 12.

"Five!" . . . So Time now expresses itself from midnight to midnight
in groups of four digits ranging from 0001 to 2400,
and is to be so designated on all dispatches, orders,
reports, messages and bulletins pertaining to operations in the field.
"Get set, men." The captain's arm drops. "0600. Let's go!"

Would there be armies if clocks had never been invented?

The boatswain's corrugated voice is heard over the loudspeaker system.
"Boat team number five—repeat, five—form at station three."
You find your feet and they move you toward the
rail of the transport and your shadow joins the men
crowding their quickened bodies in orderly and predetermined lines and
scraping their heavy shoes in a gruff shuffle of expectancy.

Your ears sting as the guns of the task force
resume their nightlong exploration of the dim island lying ahead,
sending out an expedition of sixteen, eight and five-inch shells
to trace its fugitive boundaries and map them in thunder
and record the charted areas in red and yellow smoke.

Empty Higgins boats, Alligators and the more sturdily armed Buffaloes
scurry about the mother ship in busy clouds of spray
like fat little infant pigs eagerly waiting to be suckled.
Soldiers are going over the side in groups of four
and their white knuckles grasp the vertical strands of netting.

There goes Egan, Whitney, Shearer and the kid called Mouse.
The first men in the craft hold the net inside
to prevent anyone from falling between the boat and ship.
Your turn soon. A man behind you coughs. Another swears.
The man you follow has a face like embalmed youth.

Now . . . You climb over the ship's rail, clutching at rope,
feeling the swaying ladder with tentative toes, somehow not yours.
It writhes with the weight of bodies above and below
and it snaps and plunges in whirling heights of dizziness.
Then your flexed muscles grow taut and they bend back
the water and the sky and the elements and they
drop you into the craft like a jigsaw puzzle piece
fitted into its proper place to complete the desired pattern.

The assault boat is full of men pressed close together.
Someone says, "Guess we'll have to breathe in half steps!"
But his voice sounds strangely unlubricated and out of practice.

You read an unanswerable question in the eyes of Egan,
and you wonder if he sees the same in yours.
And everyone looks at everyone else as though each man
were trying to gather in the nearness of his fellows
for strength against a loneliness that might come too soon.

The engines roar in the opening bars of a symphony
and a scream of trumpets leaps from the feverish hull.
The chorus of waves rises to a sustained andante
and the kettledrums of shifting equipment roll in irregular counterpoint,
each measure ending in a cymbalstroke of thumping rifle butts.
Then the theme is developed with solos of baritone profanity
softly accompanied by the delicate plucking of a stringed prayer.

You are moving up and down with the rushing breakers
as though you are being carried on a great pendulum
whose accelerating momentum is completely out of your personal control—
the ultimate cycle, the last swing from ship to shore,
with an insignificant little clot of humanity balanced in between.

You watch the transport fade slowly away in dazzlepainted aloofness
and your mind twists itself in a grimace of recollection.
You remember the embarkation point somewhere in the South Pacific.
You remember sweating out the line waiting to go aboard,
the muggy, airless ship's mess where you ate standing up,
the cramped quarters below where you fitfully tried to sleep,
and nights when fear would come to bed with you,
stroking your face with hot fingers, urging her thighs close
while her head hung down heavily on your convulsing throat
and her hair caught in your breath and you choked . . .

This is the best cure for wanting to go abroad.

There is a faint drizzle and the pulsating lagoon seems
to be puppeted from above by thin wires of wetness.
A flippant breeze dances along the gunwale, finding casual amusement
in splitting each moment open and daintily quaffing its kernel
and tossing the shells in your face with light contempt.

At rendezvous points columns of boats swerve in wide arcs
aimed at the outlying tentacles of the sprawling enemy octopus,
intending to paralyze with simultaneous hatchet blows in many places.
Some are diversionary in character, while others have special missions
like severing communication lines or capturing airstrips or demolishing instal-
        lations.

Your craft is in the third echelon approaching Beach Red.
You can see the island now—a weird, looming blotch
shaking with violent epilepsy in the tremulous haze of dawn.

There is sickeningly green water beating itself in frothing desperation,
trying to escape the restraining ministrations of reef and sandbar,
and lurching in giddy drunkenness and vomiting on its clothes.
There is the rich, resonant cough of the Navy's guns,
as trim cruisers and destroyers clear their throats and spit,
streaming their shattering saliva into the turbulent cuspidor curving ahead.
There are carrier-based divebombers screeching like hordes of dishonored
        women,
bloodstreaking their ravishers with outraged claws of machine gun strafing,
and biting with explosive teeth and wielding lashes of flame.

You pass the control boat where the commanding brigadier general
supervises the formation, composition, direction and space between assault waves.
His staff, in bobbing amphtracks, diligently blueprint the approaching battle,
convinced that God is on the side having weightier papers.

The boat turns on the edge of your heightening suspense
and knifes into the scarred back of a rolling billow.
Your head is low, fixed stiffly to your drawn shoulders,

and you are afraid to raise it because it might
fly off like a hairspring when the pressure is released.

Your mouth is a vacuum and speech is remote and
any sound from it would be a turgid groan. Your
mind looks at itself and it shrinks away and wonders
whether or not to stand bravely or run and hide.
Feelings, senses and physical motion are faint and far off,
and all existence is a rushing wind in your ear.

The Navy coxswain in the bow splinters the brittle atmosphere
and turns to yell for the men to keep down.
They swear hoarsely but crouch lower, grateful for the interruption
and a chance to ease the tremendous activity of waiting.

Simmons cracks, "All we need now is a travel agent
distributing literature about South Sea cruises!" There is loosening laughter
and a tugging, stretching pincers lets go of your nerves.

Whitney is encouraged to wonder where the local U.S.O. is,
and Private Lloyd says that hulahula hostesses with ballbearing hips
will meet us on the beach with doughnuts and coffee.
Ivey hopes to hell they don't have grass skirts on.
"Me with my hay fever" . . . and you know those words
will never appear in weekly magazines, but you're Goddam proud.

The bottom of the Higgins boat crunches into firm coral
and heaves to a standstill. It's footwork from here in.
The steel armor plate splashes outward to form a ramp
and the men mass forward in a lump of courage.

You are only about forty yards from the beach line
and you can see the white nakedness of the sand
exposed here and there under its negligee of lacy smoke.
Sergeant Lindstrom is the first to leap into the surf,
riding the breakers on the crest of a cocky smile.

"All right, boys. Leave us look good in the newsreels!"

Men on the righthand side of the landing craft disembark
over the front corner of the ramp and step off
to the right oblique, while those on the opposite side
move similarly to the left. The coxswain keeps the engines
purring in order to prevent the boat from turning sideways.

Here you go. The sea accepts you with stoic indifference,
investigating your hips with routine efficiency and a practiced touch
and emptying the warmth from the pockets of your body.

Draw in your breath. Hold your piece at high port.
Keep moving. Churn through the foam. Don't try to run
or the drag of the waves will upset your balance.
Proceed diagonally to the swirling surf with feet wide apart.

The overhead barrage covering the landing sounds like the screech
of a jalopy's brakes before it crashes into a barn.
Shell bursts stride across the atoll roof with awkward boots
and towers of orange flame spring up in their footprints.
A fifty-pound projectile from a five-inch Navy gun swoops down
and a leaping tree smears its green across the sky.

You see the men of the first two attacking waves
swarming up on the beach, digging in or creeping ahead.
Mortar units go forward to blast pathways through the strongpoints,
and the supporting fire of rifle squads can be heard
crackling like the stiff pages of newspapers bearing death notices.

Walk out your life from one step to the next
because that's all you can be sure of. Oh, Christ,
wouldn't it be nice to lie in the gurgling tide,
limp, cool and unknowing like the simple end of everything?

You wonder why there is no fire from the defenders.
Where is the spew of 37-mm. cannon raking the boats,
the heavy machine guns, the howitzers and small arms fire,

the shrapnel from AA guns leveled off at point blank?
Will this be a relatively undefended island? Have the Japs
abandoned their shore positions in favor of higher ground inland?
Or are they waiting for the right moment . . . just waiting?

You are surprised to find that you can think clearly
and that all your senses have suddenly become extraordinarily perceptive.
You smell salt air mixed with the odor of cordite
and you can taste the curdled roots of your tongue.

Ahead of you are jagged bits of concrete strewn around—
the shattered remnants of obstacle blocks sunk in reefs offshore,
and straggling along the sand above the high tide mark
are the shapeless parings of a double apron barbed wire
entanglement with now and again torn extremities dipped in craters.

Look out! Quick calamity, let loose by the meagre pressure
of a brown digit stabs the surf ten feet away.
Snipers! The first bullet ever fired at you in anger!
My God—there's another! A squirming little dagger of lead
kicks up the wet sand rising in front of you.

Terror cracks its bristling whip as you mount the earth
and you run astride of the breeze with no awareness
of your feet touching ground. Nothing but the void consciousness
of being relentlessly exposed and caught in a cone of
suction that pulls you helplessly back into its deserted vortex.

Hit the dirt! Sink your knees in the shuddering sand.
Fling out your elbows and let your extended rifle butt
absorb the punch of sudden breathlessness. Now roll, roll, roll.
Thrust your meat outward and spin on your belching bowels,
once, twice, in the mad twitch of some agonized dreamer.
Lie still. A nightmarish hangover is sitting on your eyelids.

You got up on the wrong side of the world.

Rejoice, O young man, in thy youth (Keep down, down.
Rest your body on your legs and on your arms
and for Jesus' sake don't let your pimply ass protrude.
Cradle your rifle in the bends of your two elbows
high enough so that no sand gets in the muzzle.
Now place your hands out in front of your head,
lift your belly and your chest slightly off the ground
and drag your carcass along by pulling with the wrists.
Crawl, dammit—not like a snake, but like a baby.)

And let thy heart cheer thee (So here you are,
of all the innumerable millions of men now and before,
at all the crowded intersections on the roadmap of eternity,
you and you only, placed by war's shifting of furniture
on this barren square foot of a condemned property island
to cover the spot where the rug's a little worn.
No, you don't have to fight. There's no compulsion whatever.
Nobody's talking themselves red, white and blue in the face
and only the sea is behind you if you turn.
It's just you and your firearm, the enemy and his,
and a perfectly democratic opportunity to use your own judgment.)

Walk in the ways of thine heart (Get up, now.
This is where you take the tags off your uniform.
Watch your step, and remember to shoot when anything moves
and move when anything shoots. Where are the little bastards?
Where are the orphans of heaven screaming, "American, you die!"
or "Iki, waki, konki, sookekki!"—spirit, harmony, stamina, total action!?
Nothing but trees wearing their hair parted in the middle
and sandalwood and frangipani and sago plants and sour mud
and camouflage suits mingling with foliage like visiting poor relations
and bullets sounding as though harpstrings were being impatiently tugged.)

And in the sight of thine eyes (Here are events
visibly projected in a changing kaleidoscope pattern of raw technicolor.
You see greenpainted faces and they are stifled with caution

as men advance in the mounting strain of sound effects.
There is quick, whirring action in a riot of noise
and darkness follows light, blinding the jerky blur of finality
as death turns over another page and resumes its commentary.
There is the crisp contour of destruction in startling sequence
and a corpse with its tongue stuck out at civilization
melts dimly away in a cross texture of coming attractions.
And the actors become stagestruck, stammer and forget their lines
because the script has suddenly demanded that they interpret reality.)

Yea, if a man live many years (Look. There's Mouse,
pushing a stern expression before him as he goes forward.
The calendar slapped him on the back and offered laughter
and pretty ankles and hot swing records and seats on
the 50-yard line and a coke at the corner drugstore . . .
And what of it, if no one will ever say
that this island battle was won on the playing fields
of Pembroke Junior College?) *Let him rejoice in them all.*

But let him remember the days of darkness. (The past
is beyond your influence, the present is something about which
you can do nothing, and the future is a mixture
of both. Let the guns argue about it among themselves.
Let the sand and the water debate as to who
shall extinguish your faltering flicker of life. And let time
break it into its component parts and pack them separately
and ship by express to the other side of tomorrow
and put the pieces together.) *For they shall be many.*

God will protect idiots, drunkards and Americans. It's His profession.

There are three battalions in the force attacking Beach Red,
plus complements of artillery, combat engineers and several armored elements.
The detachment is to advance to a designated assembly point,
dig in and wait for further orders to push on.

Your platoon is deployed to right and left of you
in open squad columns, with six feet between each man.
Everyone is tense and soberly dignified—like a solemn procession
of the Benevolent and Protective Order of the Sweaty Palm.

Up ahead, Yanks appear and vanish between clots of vegetation,
and rifles extend their sharpnailed fingers and crack their knuckles.
Fierce rebuttals result and machine guns cry out, "Da-da-dat! Da-da-dat!"
The Garand exclaims "Kapow!" and the 4.2″ mortar adds "Palot!"
while the bazooka terminates the discussion with an irrefutable "Phoosh!"

Your brain is a pincushion stuck full of pricking reminders.
Get on the ball! Look around for cover and concealment!
Think of what you're going to shoot at. Think! Think!
Will you know a Jap when you see the bastard?
What did that intelligence officer say on board the ship?
He said that you could expect anything. Anything at all.

Okay, so it's anything. Anything that's about five feet three,
wearing a pair of shorts and maybe a speckled shirt
or pajamas or maybe a full uniform or maybe nothing.
Anything that's stocky of build, with almost no perceptible waistline,
that moves around with a shuffle rather than a stride
and that has rubber soled canvas shoes on its feet
in which the big toe is separated from the others.
Anything with yellow skin inclined toward hairiness, and buck teeth
and a pair of squinting eyes slanted toward the nose
and a characteristic odor like the smell of wild animals.

Watch it! There is a spurt of Japanese rifle fire
and Bill Shearer, off to one side, staggers and crumples.

Private Whitney shouts, "The Goddam sons of bitches are underground!"
and you drop on your face, clinging to the earth.

Don't move. Don't lift your head. Japs usually fire high.
Your belly deflates itself and lies flat against your backbone.
You hear bullets slashing leaves and ripping bark from trees
and the slugs penetrate the wood with a vibrant sound
and you wonder if it is the same with flesh.

Listen. Can you tell where the shots are coming from?
Your helmet has fallen over your eyes. Raise it slightly.
Look around. See that pile of coconut fronds over there?
That's it! Watch it quiver with muzzle recoil. That's it!

Lloyd, on your right, fumbles for a hand grenade and
his voice is grated. "Let's blast 'em! Let's blast 'em!"
Your fingers feel along your waist and extract a grenade,
pressing the release lever against your hand. Get set now.
Twist your neck. Take out the pin with your teeth.
Loosen the lever. Prop yourself up with a stiff arm
and toss it wide. Watch it arch end over end,
merging with others thrown simultaneously toward the heap of rubble.
They land near the target. One rolls a few feet.
Then they explode and the doors of hell clang open.

The men are up, rushing forward with their pieces poised.
A dark silhouette squirms from the hole and wriggles away,
and rifles count quicktime cadence. It slumps and lies still.

Egan reaches the debris of the position and he pukes.
Others stand staring with their mouths open and eyes glazed.
You feel ill and fevered and reality has become hallucination
and hallucination is the only thing that has become real.

You have stumbled into history and can't get out again.

Here are the cleft ends and chips of human wood
hacked asunder by the cleantoothed axe of instant death, lying
around in new sap with their split terminals curled up.

You see a stray foot with a shoe still on
and a head with a cigarette still between its teeth.
And here's a dead Jap, miraculously whole, propped stiffly erect
as though waiting for his officer to say, "At ease!"

The brief storm of grenades has uncovered a spider trench
cleverly connected by hidden underground passages to its subterranean twin,
so that when you look inside, the hole appears empty
and you pass on into the sights of a rifle
jutting from those disheveled palm fronds aimed at your back.

You begin to realize the stealthy nature of the Nip
and you appreciate how painstakingly he has organized the terrain.
You are deeply thankful for the barrage preceding the attack,
and for the dugouts uprooted and the gun positions obliterated
and the Japs relegated to the status of honorable ancestors.

Lt. Nixon waves and yells, "Don't bunch up, you guys!
You're a perfect home for a mortar shell. Keep moving!"
He points to a large rock about fifty yards away
and tells the men to stop when they reach it
in order to properly reorganize for the next cautious advance.

A sniper opens up with the pingping of his .25
and a Yank with a Tommy rushes across the grass
and pauses at the foot of a tree and peers
upward and holds his weapon in an ironic 'present arms'
and salutes the enemy in a final courtesy of lead.

All around you the fighting seems to flare up again.
Japs boil from dugouts like scum rising to the surface

and are ladled off by timely employment of sanitary utensils
and are consigned to refuse before damage can be done.

Look! There's a slithering brown figure behind those mangrove leaves.
Quick! Raise your rifle to your shoulder and take aim.
Shoot him! Attaboy, you blew his nuts off. Shoot again,
the bastard's still kicking. You got him! You got him!

You feel like a babbling halfwit, light and unthinking, as
though you had dipped your reason in flowing blood and
mopped it over your bones and wrung it out and
tossed it for the wind to wear in its hair.

The clump of trees ahead is fuming with rattling gunfire
and it sounds like a forest full of rolling dice.
Come seven. Come eleven. Wheel 'em. Monk 'em. Pass. Fade.
Men are speculating. Some make their point. Others crap out.

And what of the dead? What of those distorted remnants,
those foul, blistered torsos from the rice paddies of Formosa,
those bloated ghosts gone back to the smoke of Fujiyama,
those stepchildren of the Emperor, lately of Honshu or Nagasaki?
Do they feel the swooning heat or the suffocating dampness
or tigers in their intestines or tissue drowning in sweat,
or the sickness, the retching, the drooling, the trembling desolation?

Well, then, who dares compare the simple ease of death
to the agony of living under the strain of battle,
when your eyes leer into the ugly countenance of despair
and your ears deafen themselves to a wounded friend's cry
because the assault must be made strictly according to schedule
and what matter the fallen crumbs from the military timetable;
when your battered soul becomes a dispossessed and separate self,
forgetting the body that bore it, claiming only remote kinship
with a slobbering mouth and hands ashen with fused hatred?

Murder is your sixth sense. You lost the other five.

The principal assault has already taken place on Beach Blue
to the west of the island, and it seems apparent
that the enemy has retreated to his previously prepared defenses.

Heavy guns blare out their syncopated jazz and abruptly stop
and there is a short pause while the warring spirits
terminate their jitterbugging and stand around to applaud the number.
Then someone puts another nickel in the same old jukebox
and havoc selects a partner and the dance goes on.

Enfilading fire from the Jap positions on high terrain inland
whines over your head on its way to the beach,
trying to impede the bringing up of supplies and artillery
and knock out the tanks that LSTs are disgorging offshore.

Your skin is split with alertness and with every explosion
your spine runs up your back, cowering between your shoulders.
Your thoughts as you advance are absurdly out of character
and they form in single file in your mind and
they shove and they bump in an effort to get
away while escapes are still plainly marked, so they can
march across your body in wondering pity. Well, let them
out. Let everything that you have ever heard and everything
that you have ever been taught squeeze itself free so
that what you have left is what you really know.

Be careful. The danger of a counterattack is always present.
The Japanese system of defense is based largely on maneuver.
They do not resist energetically, but yield with the blow,
intending to hit back unexpectedly and decisively when the attacker
has been disorganized by the extent of his own penetration.
And they do not withdraw without leaving harassing elements behind
in the form of isolated strongpoints and special rearguard troops.

In front of you is a fringe of matted vegetation,
and the push slows down. There is no precision here,

no formation of steadily advancing men. Just an unhealthy mixture
of friend and foe stirred vigorously in a seething caldron.

Beyond is the jungle's steaming pie, fresh from the oven,
with a stinking coagulation of mud and water as filling
under a hard, unyielding crust of firmly tangled tropical foliage—
the whole gripped in the hand of some malicious comedian
ready to fling it in your face and exit laughing.

The leader of a forward patrol drops back to report
that an elaborately fortified center of resistance lies just ahead,
solidly emplaced, well sited, with lanes of fire skillfully cut
and ringed about by machine gun nests and individual ratholes.

The company is halted and Captain MacDonald regroups the platoons.
He appoints additional scouts to move ahead of the troops,
sending still others to each flank for security and control.
He tells the men to watch every step they take
and warns them to be sure to retain squad contact.
Then he turns back to talk earnestly over the radiophone,
and you hear the rumble of tanks on the beach.

You know that unsupported small arms cannot breach strong positions,
and you wonder how the operation is going to develop.
You've heard of Jap bunkers covered with gasoline and burned
and sealed with dirt only to hold out for days.
Ordinary grenades and even mortars are useless against these pillboxes
because the superstructures are reinforced with sturdy, sandfilled steel drums
and the entrances are angled to trap a grenade's burst.

The roar of the tanks behind you is becoming louder,
and as you creep onward through the tall Kunai grass
you feel the ground beginning to tremble with approaching thunder.

Weather prediction: Light tanks followed by Infantry. Probably scattered Japs

The Nips seem to have dug pits into the slope
of a slight incline, probably reinforcing their compact earthen breastworks
with sheets of thick iron and revetments of palm logs.
There are slits through which the mouths of cannon speak,
announcing with blustering arrogance that all trespassers will be prosecuted,
while vehement machine guns add their singsong gibberish in agreement.

Camouflaged bunkers, built on the jungle floor, border the position,
and an outer edging of obstacles contributes its further protection.
You can see trees piled up to form an abatis
and shallow trenches containing 'gooseberries' and 'concertinas' of barbed wire,
and you make out upright entanglements strung through the brush
with tin cans tied at intervals to give the alarm.

Here come the tanks, waddling like slaphappy wrestlers, brutal and
crazed, with their bellies rumbling in an effort to digest
their fuel. They lumber on unsteady treads and vent their
fury by blindly felling young trees with wild, dissolute haymakers.

You see one, then another, then two more lunging forward,
shrugging off a spatter of bullets, recoiling, turning around groggily,
then crouching to charge with their teeth shrieking shrill invective.

As a preliminary, they saturate the area with huge cartridges
that serve up deadly shrapnel fragments on the half shell,
tempting the customers with generous portions and loud sales talk.

Then their 37-mm. guns grow tired of the gastronomic dilettantism
and tear back the lips of the pillboxes' twisted mouths
and force down the main dish of hot, scorching destruction.

The position directly in front of you has been silenced,
and as the tanks turn to peddle their delicacies elsewhere,
a combat engineer unit punctually arrives to present the check.

Two men spring up to lay a heavy, pungent smokescreen
that swirls in the heat like the ectoplasm of forgotten

warriors. Wire cutters snip a jagged aisle through the entanglement
and others set off bangalore torpedoes to complete the thoroughfare.

Then the men with flame throwers dart through the opening
and inscribe their invitations to hell on ignited sheets while
specialists in persuasion set off insistent postscripts of TNT and
slip the blocks through embrasures in the bunker and address
them to whom it may concern, signed, sealed and delivered.

A Jap runs out of the ruins, his uniform ablaze,
and cartridges popping from the ammo belt around his waist.
The engineer wheels and aims his nozzle and presses the
trigger plate on the top of the barrel of his
M1-A1 apparatus. A stream of livid fuel spurts like a
fiery rod and describes a trajectory as cleancut as a
tracer bullet, searing the Nip till his entrails ooze pink.

You hear two short, sharp blasts of Lt. Nixon's whistle
and your heart stutters but you rise with bayonet ready.

The air is sticky with smoke and flame and wreckage,
and the earth feasts on a macabre pot of flesh.
Here is a victory garden of ripe corpses, grinning heads
like rounded cabbage and arms and legs in natural disorder
stained with the bright juice of tomatoes, plump and petulant.

A dirty limb twitches under a pile of lifelessness and
you stab it and it stops and lays limply . . . No,
don't reserve space in the obituary column of tomorrow's *Times*
until you are certain that all bodies are suitably extinct.
These gentlemen of Japan have a highly developed national talent
for looking the part of cadavers—realistically true to death.

Lindstrom prods enemy remains with his bayonet and on his
face you see an expression of extreme revulsion and distaste.

"Hell," says the sergeant, "killing Japs isn't war. It's K.P.!"

As it is written, there is none righteous, not one
(Here is a young Jap who had his "sennimbari" on—
sash of a thousand stitches—guaranteed to give its wearer
luck, courage, long life and complete immunity from American bullets.
Japanese Patriotic Women's Association members stand on busy street corners
and ask everyone who passes to make a single stitch
so that a thousand persons help to make one belt.)

They are all gone out of the way. (In the
beginning, everything was as nothing. And then in the Plain
of High Heaven there were gods who lived in quietness
for long years. One day there came a male god
called Izanagi, and he dipped his spear into the deeps,
and when he withdrew it the great drops that fell
from his jeweled weapon formed the sacred Islands of Japan.)

They are together become unprofitable. (Then were his eyes cast
upon Izanimi, a female goddess, who greeted him with favor,
and in the August Presence they became man and wife.
However, their children were not good, and by celestial divination
it was found that there had been a grave error
in the wedding ceremony; the male, and not the female,
should have been the first to speak to the other.
So the marriage was repeated, with Izanagi opening the conversation,
thus assuring the superiority of the male for all time.)

There is none that doeth good. (Among their numerous progeny,
born when Izanagi washed his honorable nose, was one Susano-O,
who was called the God of Swift Impetuous Male Augustness.
He was rough and uncontrollable, of violent and irrepressible spirits,
and it is from him that the manhood of Japan
is said to have derived its individual and racial character.)

Their throat is an open sepulchre (This chunk of youth
whose erupted mouth slops its spittle into the torn sand,
was he not taught in early boyhood that his life

had one holy purpose above all others: to identify itself
with the personality and the behavior of his native land
and thus to live forever with an eternal Japanese soul?)

With their tongues they have used deceit. (They gave him
a military uniform at twelve, and he learned to recite,
"If I fight at sea my body will be embalmed
by the salt waves. If I fight in the hills
my body will be changed into moss. But only one
thing matters—to die a hero's death for the Emperor.")

*The poison of asps is under their lips whose mouth
is full of cursing* (Later on, at his training center,
he was issued a rifle—a "Meiji 38th Year" model—
with the whole company drawn up on the parade grounds
and the commanding officer addressing it on the honor bestowed.
As his name was called, he came forward, bowed low,
accepted the gun and raised it ritualistically to his forehead.
Then he stepped back, presented arms, and resumed his place.)

And the ways of peace have they not known. (From
then on he lived in accordance with a strict code
covering many pages of very involved logic in fine print.
This reminded him that duty was heavier than a mountain
while death was lighter than a feather, and that loyalty
and devotion were standard equipment wherever he might find himself.
It urged him to be severe in observing due propriety,
demanding that he make simplicity his aim, avoiding frivolous luxuries,
and informed him that the orders of a superior officer
were to be construed as emanating from the Emperor himself.)

And before he left home he conducted his own funeral.

The platoon passes on into the thicket and Lt. Nixon
orders the men to keep a sharp lookout for snipers.
He steps on a game trail leading into the interior
and motions for the leading squad to fall in behind.

You scrutinize the bark of the trees all around you
for the telltale notches that snipers make to facilitate climbing,
and vigilance enters your mind and collects in the corners
and your thoughts contract themselves into beads that you twist
on a tenuous string with no knot at the end.

Oh, hell—why search for something that you can't see?
Why be afraid of pain that you may never feel?
Battle is a huge clockwork and your squad is one
of its little wheels and every time the hands meet
they pinch off another bit of existence. It's a force
that keeps driving you on and you can't control it,
so add up your chances and throw away the result.

The winding lane angles off into a muddy stream bed
and the column takes more interval and eyes become expectant.
And then, with the unwelcome drama of dreaded fulfillment, there
is a spasm of sound and a bullet's smarting splash
and Mouse clutches at his hip and goes down groaning.

The Lieutenant cries, "Get off the trail! Hurry! Take cover!"
You leave the path and crash into the bordering undergrowth.

Mouse is bleeding in a crimson spread from his thigh
and is shocked at what he sees but cannot believe.
Lindstrom tries to worm his way toward the wounded man,
but Lt. Nixon grabs his shoulder, saying, "For Christ's sake
don't go out there! The bend is covered. It's suicide!
Where's a medic? Send a medic up here right away!"

Four men are detailed to make a wide circling movement
and approach the sniper's suspected position from several different points

and their helmets and splotch uniforms disappear into the foliage
and you see curses forming on compressed and clamped mouths.

Here comes one of the company medical corpsmen and he
coolly crawls out into the open trail where Mouse lies.
He doesn't wear a red cross brassard—no aidman does—
since the Jap snipers deliberately select them as choice targets.

Your rifle is poised to shoot at any suspicious flurry
in surrounding trees and your vision is halved by the
spectacle of the medic's approach and the danger above him
and you watch the clumsy geometry of a body suffering.

He reaches Mouse and with a deft and practiced motion
pulls him around to face in the direction of safety.
Then he firmly loops his wrists under the boy's armpits
and with a bizarre exhibition of swimming on dry land
drags the casualty back to cover behind a convenient log.

He sprinkles sulfa powder on the wound and he takes
the prepared bandage out of Mouse's first aid pouch and
rips away the shredded trouser and patches him with gauze.
Then he takes out his hypodermic and removes the shield
and prepares the needle and syrette, and breaks the seal
and punctures the skin of Mouse's arm in a diagonal
thrust and squeezes the tube, withdrawing the needle. Next, he
extracts a tag and prepares to note all the information
so that the battalion aid station may be guided accordingly
when the litter bearers take the man to the rear.

The medic says, "We've got some pretty fair pillrollers, kid,
and if you haven't got more than thirty bullet holes
there ain't a Goddam thing for you to worry about."

Gallantry isn't written of or talked about. It is done.

The shots of the men searching for the sniper engrave
a random motif in the texture of jungle growth as
soldiers penetrate the dubious uncertainty of each puff of verdure
and cross-examine the shrubs that cannot offer a satisfactory accounting.

Excitedly one of the stalkers calls out, "I see him!
I see the lousy monkey! Up there in that tree!"
You thrash toward the voice and you see Private Simmons
gliding intently across the trail with rifle at shoulder level.

While the others remain in concealment to cover his approach,
he kneels and raises his piece and takes aim and
fires and the noise reverberates in whirlpools of expanding echo.

There is a crush of twigs and a camouflaged figure
hurtles along an irregular chute of foliage, arms helplessly flailing,
and lands face down with a hollow thump of finality.

Private Simmons follows the body's fall with his rifle barrel,
then fires again and again into the impotent, desolate enemy.
He runs forward, stitching the air with his weaving bayonet
and pinions the supine figure, twisting it on its back.

He is rigid with consternation. "Dammit, this ain't no Jap.
It's a dummy! Look—there's a rope tied to it!
It's a dummy!" He turns around in puzzlement. "A dummy!"

Simmons does not hear the report of the Jap 6.5 mm.
and his mouth is still wide with speech and mystery
when the bullet rips into his chest. He half turns
and pitches in an inert fold across the decoy carcass.

Graham comes charging out from under his covering of grass
and his lips are a thin slit of bitter fury
as he sights his BAR at a wreath of smoke
and empties his clip in a falsetto of hysterical laughter.

A rifle slithers to the ground. It's a Jap 97.
Graham starts for it, but Lt. Nixon suspects another trick.
"Get back! Get back!" he calls. Graham doesn't stop. He
indicates the weapon and he says, "There's blood on it,
fresh blood. By God, he's hanging by his blue balls!"

You look up at the spectral outline of a form
smudged with gore and bent double in an ungainly caricature,
and suspended by a belt lashed to the palm trunk.
"Cut it down, somebody," says the Lieutenant, and Pfc. Chapman
draws his trench knife and prepares to climb the tree.

The sniper's firearm is lying with its butt partially imbedded.
A metal tube with fluted baffles, about eight inches long
is fixed to the muzzle, and you think to yourself,
So that's why the blast was so chopped and scattered.

Sgt. Lindstrom picks it up and examines it with curiosity.
He thumbs back the bolt and takes out a bullet.
"Man, oh, man! These are explosive. When they hit anything
they sound like machine-gun bursts. Why, he could have
fired these things at rocks and logs all around us
and we'd swear to high heaven that we were ambushed!"

You wonder about the dummy. How was it let down?
Your eyes follow the twisted rope up into the tree
and then over across to the sniper's nest. A pulley!
And if the squad had passed after it was lowered,
it would have been drawn right back up into place.

Chapman warns, "Look out below!" and the body tumbles down
in a rattle of equipment. There is a gas mask,
mosquito netting, sacks of rice, concentrated food, water purifying chemicals,
some spare socks, gloves, roll and triangular bandages, a rotating-lens
flashlight, a wire eye screen, and a messkit—all bloodsoaked.

Some Japs are good losers. Others go right on living.

The platoon reforms and gets set to move inland again.
The trail has become full of haphazard twists and turns,
with holes bulging with rain and unexpected rises and declines
and mud that tries to suck the bottoms from shoes.
It has narrowed perceptibly and grown more lush and untidy
as though wearied of the constant chore of keeping house
against the encroachments of a careless and unruly jungle family.

You doubt if there will be danger from snipers now,
because an overhead maze of leafage shuts out the light
and visibility is reduced to the scrubby gorse under foot
and to the slim bamboo shoots striking at your face.

Your hearing is dimmed, for the dense vegetation absorbs sound,
but you are aware of the smells of rotting plants,
the odor of game and the musky aroma of earth.

This is the home of the wallaby, phalanger and echidna
and other fauna you have never even heard of before.
There is a bird that sounds like a demented man
banging two blocks of wood together in a moronic cacophony,
and there is another that cries like a dog barking.
Here's where fruit-bats and reptiles of all shapes and sizes
establish a free government for themselves and for their posterity . . .
And did you know that a cassowary resembles an emu?

A man five yards ahead halts and raises his arm.
The soldier in front of you performs a similar gesture
and you carry the signal back in the same way.
You turn to Ivey and ask him what's going on
and he says that he is a stranger here himself.

The men stand in a single column, at close intervals,
patiently, as though they had all the time there is.
Close your eyes and you might be in line anywhere.
It might be a chow formation or a supply line

or a payroll line or a line for cholera inoculations
or a line waiting for a bus out of camp
or any of those interminable lines you experienced during training.

The Army taught you to wait in line like this
and developed the technique to a fine art, a science.
You have been conditioned through months of waiting to believe
that nothing can happen to you while standing in line.

That's all it ever is—waiting, waiting, waiting—either at
the front or at base areas and doing odd jobs
and wondering why you are doing them, and thinking of
the utter ridiculousness of the whole situation and thinking of
home and of people you know and want to be
with again and people you don't know yet but can't
get away from. It's all people, people, people. There are
people you love and people you fight with and people
you stand in line behind. And yet it's people you
intend to kill or who will kill you if the
opportunity comes. Why in hell can't people just be people?

The column winds forward again and you wonder what's up.
Quickly the good news flits backward from man to man.
The command post just ahead . . . Assembly positions have been reached . .
Defenses established . . . The first and second echelons already digging in . .
No, don't think of it in terms of mission accomplished.
It's just a break, a respite, a chance to relax . . .
And your feelings lift in a rising barometer of relief.

The trail flows reluctantly into a sabana, ringed with trees
and miraculously free of banyan and broom and thorny creepers
and it's full of a thousand carbon copies of yourself.

"A good soldier doesn't have to rest. He can simulate."

*Behold, your dwelling shall be the fatness of the earth
and the dew of heaven from above; by the sword
shall you live and in such manner serve your brother.*

*There was a multitude of slain and a great number
of carcasses, and there was no end of their corpses . . .
For in our anger we have slain many of them
and in our selfwill we have digged down a wall . . .
Yea, we have heaped mischiefs upon them, we have spent
our arrows upon them; they were devoured with burning heat
and with bitter destruction . . . and it shall come to pass
that we shall break their yoke from off our necks.*

"Oh, my Lord, oh, my Lord, I am not eloquent,
but am slow of speech and of a slow tongue . . .
You are the Commanding Officer . . . my might and the beginning
of my strength, the excellency of dignity and of power . . .
And to the calling of Your roll I yet say,
'Lord, here am I, and thank Thee for all things.' "

"But what of the others—my brethren? What of them?
Who among them hath woe? Who hath sorrow? Who hath
babbling? Who hath wounds without cause, redness of the eyes?
Can You see their countenances, can You hear their voices?"

Lindstrom! . . . *Verily, the flakes of his flesh are joined together.
They are firm upon him and they cannot be moved.
His heart is as firm within him as a stone . . .*
"Lord, here am I, and thank Thee for all things."

Shearer! . . . *There is no healing of his bruise. His wound
is grievous. Let all the earth keep silence before him.*

Egan! . . . *Behold, he hath scouted the dominion and he cometh
leaping upon mountains, he cometh, and skipping upon the hills.*
"Lord, here am I, and thank Thee for all things."

Whitney! . . . *Yea, thou art he whom thy brethren shall praise.*
Thy hand shall be in the neck of thine enemies.
"Lord, here am I and thank Thee for all things."

Mouse! . . . *My bowels, my bowels! Oh, my Lord, I am*
pained at my very heart, and my heart doth make
a noise in me and I cannot hold my peace . . .

Graham! . . . *He is the rock and his work is perfect,*
for all his ways are the ways of his judgment.
"Lord, here am I, and thank Thee for all things."

Mason! . . . *His visage was so marred more than any man*
and his form more so than the sons of man . . .

Ivey! . . . *Lo, he that dasheth in pieces is come up*
before Thy face; keep the munition and watch the way,
and make thy loins strong and fortify thy power mightily.
"Lord, here am I, and thank Thee for all things."

Lloyd! . . . *The whole head is sick, the whole heart faint*
from the sole of the foot even unto the head.
There is no soundness in it but wound . . . and yet,
"Lord, here am I, and thank Thee for all things."

Simmons! . . . *Man that is born of a woman is of*
few days and full of trouble. Lo, he cometh forth
like a flower and is cut down; also, he fleeth
as a shadow and continueth not. Yea, he giveth up
the ghost and where is he? As the waters fail
from the sea and the river decayeth and drieth up,
so he hath layed him down and he riseth not . . .

Chapman! . . . *Behold, he standeth behind our wall, and he looketh*
in at the windows, he showeth himself through the lattice.
"Lord, here am I, and thank Thee for all things."

Only man, among living things, says prayers. Or needs to.

There go the supply boys lugging unwieldy boxes of ammunition
and cartons of field rations and tools and jungle equipment,
reducing the problems of military logistics to an aching back.

A group of men with rolls of white fabric tape
are laying out trails to guide and restrict the column,
while booby traps and trip wires are placed across approaches.
Engineers are marking a field for the planting of mines
and the circular containers are gingerly delivered to prescribed places.

Defense lines for the advanced assembly area are being disposed
in a perimeter along the outer edge of the sabana.
Squads are being allocated their positions about ten yards apart,
and sandbags are being filled and fire lanes are being
cut and observation teams are being established in nearby trees
and standing patrols are posted to cover routes of infiltration.

Melt to the ground. Turn over on your left side
and pull your canteen out of its dirtcaked canvas carrier.
Unscrew the cover and let it dangle by its chain.
Take a mouthful of water, rolling it around before swallowing,
then let its moistness trickle slowly down your parched gullet.

Funny. You always thought South Sea Island life was composed
of an exotic combination of savage headhunters and missionaries and
girls wearing sarongs in gay pursuit of one another through
picture postcard scenery. But all you've discovered so far in
this topographical error is the only place in the world
where you can stand in mud up to your bellybutton
and still have prickly silt slap you in the face . . .
Oh, well—take off your instincts and make yourself comfortable
and stretch your body out in the quiet, cool grass
and watch the hill balance the sky on its breast,
staring into the emptiness and space of its empty spaces.

Graham uncoils his lean frame at your side. He says,
"You know, I just killed a man three minutes ago.

If I lie down here long enough I'll start wondering
if maybe it wasn't the other way around." You answer,
"Forget it. Jesus Christ, forget it. Don't wonder about anything
or your brain will strip a gear. Just dial your
thoughts like a radio and tune in something entirely different."
You offer him your canteen. "Have a drink?" He shakes
his head, and he replies wryly, "If a drop of
water touched me it would probably go up in steam."

There are some casualties and they are being taken back
to the beach where pre-op cases will receive whole blood
or plasma before an amphtrack will evacuate them to ships.
Broken eggs can never be mended. They go into crates
by themselves. And how would you like to shake hands
with yourself some day and say, "Pardon my artificial extremity?"

The American dead are immovably comatose, shrouded by O.D. ponchos,
and they will be buried in accordance with Army regulations.
You think of battle orders, plans, preparations, training, maneuvers, rehearsals.
The War Department tells the Army through normal military channels
and it goes from the General Staff to the corps,
then to the division, to the regiment, to the battalion,
to the company, to the platoon and to the squad.
In tight language, bony with abbreviations and bare of adjectives,
the enemy's position is made clear and his strength inventoried.
The mission is explained with a statement of principal objectives
and a breakdown of the overall expectation into unit missions.
To this are added annexes and outlines of alternate procedures
detailing successive objectives, frontages, boundaries between detachments and
      security measures.

But nobody ever issues any instructions on how to die.

Captain MacDonald orders the men to begin digging in immediately
and you put your canteen back in its case and
unhook the harness of your combat pack and squirm free.
Then you draw out your intrenching tool from the strap
and select a site within bounds of your platoon area.

Here goes. Lie propped on your hips and start work.
Don't stand up unless you have to, because the enemy
is undoubtedly observing the clearing from positions on the hill.
Jab the small shovel into the dirt with short strokes
and place the soil in the direction of the Japs
to form a solid parapet which you will later camouflage
with oznaburg cloth of a color similar to your surroundings
or with the plentiful Kunai grass or tall brush cane.

No, it isn't very much, but you'll call it home . . .
Your parlor will be fresh soil, not yet turned mud,
with wide windows of amber sand glistening in the sun,
looking out upon the main thoroughfare of bustling community activity.
Your grounds will be broad terraces rolling in perfection and
your roof will be a towering dome of disenchanted blue
and your cellar will be a reservoir of undrinkable vintages.

Your dining room will be a knife and a spoon.
Mess kits are a nuisance unless there is hot water,
so you will eat from cans and throw them away.
Perhaps, when chow time comes, a man will open up
one of those large tins of preserved beef over there
and will cut a slice for himself with his bayonet.
Then he will replace the lid and with careful aim
and cries of "Room service!" will toss the can into
another foxhole where an adjacent epicure will await his turn.

Your bedroom, if you should sleep at all this night,
will be a shelter tent section wrapped around your body,
or a mosquito net to challenge the bearers of malaria,

with only the flat of your back for a mattress
and your belly drawn up over you for a blanket
and Stevenson's "half of a broken dream for a pillow."

Some of the men relieve the dull work of digging
by making ironic jokes on the amenities of domestic existence.
"I'm gonna write home for a set of chintz curtains,"
says Ivey. "Won't you join me for tea and bridge
tomorrow awfternoon?" asks Pvt. Chapman, his voice glutted with satire.
"So sorry, please," Ivey replies, "but I'm expecting Clare Luce."

Egan pretends to be indignant. "There's water in my basement.
I demand to see the real estate agent right away!"
"Well, you made your bed—now drink it!" laughs Whitney.
Graham points out, "You'll find the complaint department on the
eighteenth floor, two doors to your left. Take the elevator."

Lindstrom warns, "You boys better wipe your feet before entering.
I don't want any mud tracked on my clean carpet."
You say, "Why don't you transfer to the Air Corps?
There's no mud in the clouds." Ivey gasps, "Hey, fellows,
focus your 20-20s on Lt. Nixon over there. He's got
his arms dirty all the way up to his shoulderpatch.
And he once gigged me for having an unshined beltbuckle!"

Lloyd suddenly yells, "Shut up, all you guys, shut up!
Someone is trying to sneak past that row of bushes!"
He raises his rifle. There is silence. Every man drops
his shovel and reaches for his firearm. Lloyd takes aim
at a rustling branch and fires. There is agitated foliage
and a Yank from another platoon emerges red with anger.

"Can't a guy take a leak without being shot at?"

All the men let go of their muscles and laugh,
and you turn back to your digging with relief. Before
there was strain and discomfort and now a ridiculous incident
has severed the cords of the clinging hood of reticence.

Behold, how good and how pleasant it is for brethren
to dwell together in unity. As in water, face answereth
to face. So does the heart of man to man . . .

This is the aftermath, the epilogue, the period of intimacy
when men gather boldness to themselves as brooms of assurance
sweep clean the dishevelment from the threshold of their uncertainty
and dusty hands that had squeezed triggers and tossed grenades
and hurtled a clenched fist to the jaw of fear
now reach humbly out for fellowship and draw companions close
in the soft, deep communion of a great adventure shared.

The visages of men that had been wooden with intensity
and on which edged curses had whittled their rough obscenities
now open to the gossamer touch of an unashamed retrospection
and heavy doors of the mind that had swung inward
rattle on their hinges and reveal the spirit's floodlighted corridor.

Sure, it's only been a skirmish—just a minor phase
in an island campaign that really hasn't begun to begin,
and you landed on a relatively undefended strip of beach
and the enemy probably had orders to retreat before you.
But just the same, it took plenty of solid fibre
and a lot of those boys who came in ahead
will never hear anyone tell them that they were heroes . . .

You only see buckskin shirts in the movies these days,
but the sharpshooter's eye is still there, and the guts
and the insolent coolness and the large chew of tobacco.
You're exhilarated and giddy at being part of all this,
and you feel that nothing can stop you now. Nothing.

You can go out and bring back the whole universe
on the end of your bayonet and stamp it neatly
with your regimental insignia and you can lift the ocean
and all its ships and put it in your fieldpack
and you can load the stars in your rifle's chamber
and nonchalantly take some target practice at the whirling cosmos.

It's a corny feeling and a hammy feeling and a
kidstuff feeling to be able to look anyone straight in
the eye and say, "Hell, man—I was there, too."
But it's a strong feeling and it's a big feeling
and you see it reflected in the men around you.

They've got to make noise. Any kind of a noise.
It's as natural as the desire to sing tuneless serenades
after they have gone out and gotten themselves stinking drunk.
So men talk. Men from other platoons in the company,
digging in on your flank, are letting their tongues wander
about to gather up the loose bits of battle experience
and tie them together with the knotted thread of conversation . . .

"Them little slopeheads were either drugged or dizzy as hell.
I shot one and he wouldn't even look at me.
He just kept walking and walking until he toppled over."

"The Jap bastard went up in flames, like tissue paper.
Christ, Jimmy, did you ever see a human body burn?
Everything goes poof except the skull and the knee caps.
But the insides don't burn. They just pop and sizzle."

"You should have seen Jonesy. He found a few Japs
hiding in some trees. He comes back yelling, 'Coconut grove!
Coconut grove!' over and over again like he was crazy.

"And here I always thought it was just a nightclub!"

"I'm walking along and all of a sudden I come
mug to mug with two of the sons of bitches.
They turn and then start running away, like scared rats
and I take a grenade and throw it after them.
They're just a little too far out of my range,
but the explosion seems to make them groggy and confused
because they turn right around and run straight toward me,
and all I have to do is stand and shoot."

"My, my, what a hero you are. Why, I'll bet
that girl of yours will be mighty proud of you
when she marches down the church aisle with that 4-F!"

". . . So this stinking Jap comes out of his hole
and lays there rolling in the dirt begging for water.
One of our guys thinks he's got himself a prisoner
and strolls over with his canteen to toast the occasion.
As soon as he gets near enough, the little Nip
pulls the pin from a grenade stuck up his ass
and blows himself clean to hellandgone, water boy and all."

"God, yes, them Japs are tricky. We surrounded a dugout
and one of them came out carrying a white flag
and looking back and waving as though more were following.
Scottie and Chisholm got up from hiding to receive him
and then were shot down by his partners in waiting.
Kill him? Why, we tore him up in little bits. . . ."

"Those Jap snipers are mighty smooth operators. They build nests
in several trees tied together, so that when they're spotted
all they have to do is cut the trees loose
and sit back and laugh while we try to decide
which one of the trees they are actually up in."

"Hell, you ain't seen nothing. The one us boys got
had a long vine tied to a clump of grass

on one end and to a bush on the other.
The little muffdiver located himself in a tree in between
and took the middle of the vine up with him.
Then when we started shooting he pulled on the vine
as though there were men behind the bush and grass.
We sure wasted plenty of lead before we found him. . . ."

"You should have been with us. Ours had a mortar
with its mount lashed to the limb of a tree.
He kept lobbing shells at us from about 500 yards
and even had a special telephone up there with him
so he could tell his friends how he was doing."

". . . You know, when I was training back in the States,
I just barely qualified on the range with the M-1.
I guess I just didn't give a damn about shooting—
those positions they made me fire from were too uncomfortable.
But out here I shot the way I wanted to,
without using the sling or holding my breath before squeezing,
or worrying about where my elbows, wrists and legs were . . .
And boy, I got six Japs out of nine shots."

"Don't kid yourself. Those guys are plenty hard to hit.
Sometimes they'll lay out there and snap bamboo sticks together
or pull their bolts back just to draw your shots.
And they keep digging in all the time under fire
and if they get three shovelfuls loose, they're no targets."

". . . I found an abandoned machine gun in pretty good shape
so I turned it to the enemy and started shooting.
That barrel got so damn hot it blistered my hands
but I wouldn't leave it go for love or money.

"You see, it made a singing noise like mother's teakettle!"

". . . They met our line of skirmishers out in the open
and we let 'em have it with our Tommy guns.
We started to charge and the bastards turned and ran
with us whooping it up and hotfooting it after them.
All of a sudden they threw themselves on the ground
and we ran right smack into some machine gun fire
from prepared positions in their rear. God, it was awful.
Before we could flatten out we lost half our platoon."

"We had about as much sense of direction as an
eggbeater. We would chase them back and they would stop
us and maybe make us retreat a little before we
could get them started running again. And that went on
so long and over the same ground so much that
I could have picked up my own cigarette butts anytime."

"I guess I didn't have enough oil on my rifle
because the thing dried up so fast it wouldn't fire
and it started getting as hot as a witch's tit.
So I asked the Looey what in hell I ought
to do, and you know what the guy said to
me? He said, piss on it. It didn't smell very
sweet, but oh, Lordy, how that Goddam piece could shoot."

"We were cleaning up a dugout with grenades and nitrostarch,
when all of a sudden a Jap officer comes out
bloody and screaming with his face as red as a
spanked baby's ass and waving his sabre like a wildman.
He was wearing all his medals and his best uniform
and he hacked the air to bits like a windmill.
It took a lot of brass to charge that way,
and I have no doubt that a letter of commendation
will be written to the Emperor concerning his fearless act
and that he will find himself promoted in rank—posthumously."

"If I hadn't seen old Rogers with my own eyes
I never would have believed that he could do it.

We located a bunker and got down on our bellies
and moved as cautiously as a centipede with ingrown toenails.
There were five of us and we got to within
fifteen yards of the position without the Nips seeing us.
But when we opened up with our BARs and M1s
we found that we were completely surrounded by enemy nests.
They pinned us down tight with their fifties and thirties
and I began to see us listed under latest casualties.
Hot water? Well, I guess we needed a bath, anyhow.
Rogers was in a bad spot over to my left.
The Japs were using dumdum bullets in their machine guns
and I saw a couple of them hit the stock
of his rifle and slam the thing right out of
his hands. It flew about five feet into the air
and came down on his steel helmet with a bang.
We didn't know that he had been knocked out cold
until we moved for cover and he didn't follow us,
but just laid out there while the Japs took his
measùrements for a lead casket. He was nicked by fragments
and when he came to he started yelling, 'Mary! Mary!'
None of us were named Mary, so I guessed that
he was kind of delirious and was calling for his
wife. Anyway, Rogers got up and started throwing grenades around
in the cutest exhibition of one-man armies I've ever seen,
and by the time the rest of our company arrived
all those Nip buggers had enlisted in the ancestor reserve."

"Yeah, I know. These married men ain't scared of nothing."

Talk, talk, talk. You like to listen to men talk
at a time like this, because their lips seem to
bloom into ponderous slowgaited poetry and it is rich and
wholesome. The sky has been knocked loose and the cardinal
points of the compass have been jumbled in wreckage, but
they are straightening things out with their tongues and reducing
chaos to ordinary commonplace by nonchalant gestures. And it is
not a single battle they have taken part in, it
is thousands of battles and they have been fought by
thousands of men a thousand ways a thousand times over,
with everyone having a thousand versions of the same thing.

There seems to be some excitement near the Command Post,
and the men quiet down and they look and listen.
You raise yourself on one knee and see a file
of begrimed soldiers on the far side of the clearing
stumble across the matted brush, guided by a gesticulating sentry.

A young, blonde lieutenant, who seems to be in charge,
waves a curt dismissal order to the men and turns
to report to Colonel Watson in the regimental headquarters dugout.
The rest of the detachment, battered and weary, flop listlessly
down to lie in the sweat of their utter exhaustion.

One of them is near enough to hear you speak
and you try to attract his attention. "Hyah, hairy ears.
You look like you've been overdrawn at the blood bank.
What happened?" When he faces your way, you recognize him
as a member of Company A, 759th Amphibious Engineer battalion
with whom your unit had practiced assault landings on maneuvers.
"It was rough," he says. "It was rough and rugged.
A complete snafu. The sons of bitches sucked us in
and we caught everything but the Goddam boat going home."

His mouth is open and words fall out in a
tired monotone and you retrieve them and put them together

in proper sequence. He is saying that he was attached
to the division that spearheaded the attack and he hit
Beach Blue at H-hour minus thirty minutes and his mission
was to push inland and capture high ground so that
enfilading artillery support could be directed to assist following waves.

"The barrage we laid down was so strong it will
take me the rest of the day to stop vibrating.
Anyway, it sure cleaned the Japs from their shore defenses
because when we came in there wasn't hardly anyone there.
We had every kind of landing craft, including rocket-firing types,
and plenty of tanks and heavy weapons and it sure
looked like nothing on earth was going to stop us."

But the Nips were waiting behind the stretches of shoreline
and were deployed to make every man and bullet count,
and the attackers paid for every inch. Finally, they were
able to reach the foot of the hill and they
divided themselves into a lot of small teams in order
to surround the entire circle of the hill's military crest.

"We chopped our way upward, fighting for each little rise,
when WHAM! the whole world came to a screeching halt.
You know what? They were rolling landmines down on us!
Everything got fouled up, and the attack was badly stalled,
and all our rear elements had to dig themselves in.
In the confusion we got cut off from our unit
and had to find our way to your assembly area."

A passing officer stops to stare curiously at the group.
He asks, "Are you boys the refugees from Beach Blue?"

"Yes," replies one, "we spent a lifetime there this morning."

So the attack from Beach Blue has been stopped cold!
The Japs allowed the boys to land—even offered them
every encouragement to do so—but once they tried to
penetrate inland they got just so far and no farther.
You wonder what the enemy's wily little game can be.
Anyhow, this much seems clear. It won't be a pushover.
It's going to be a real battle, long and tough.

What if your forces are hemmed in on these few
hundred yards of shoreline—"contained" as the military phrasemakers say?
What then? The Japs are sure to infiltrate after dark.
It will be a long night of ceaseless small war
during which you'll discover new things about them—mostly unpleasant.
They will advance from tree to tree and make noise
and call familiar nicknames of men or yell for help.
They will crawl right up to your foxhole and drop
a hand grenade inside it and then dart quickly away . . .

Quit your bellyaching. Here comes a runner from the C.P.
He approaches Captain MacDonald and hands him a paper slip.
Maybe it's orders to move. Maybe the artillery's all set.
Maybe this deal can be put away in the cooler
before the enemy gets a chance to reorganize and counterattack.

The C.O. finishes reading the message and nears your platoon.
He announces, "I want your attention, men." They stop digging
and there is silence and everybody looks at him, trying
to extract meaning and comprehension from the set contour of
his mouth. His eyes travel along the line from face
to face and they stop at Sgt. Lindstrom and he
gestures with his head. Then he motions to Egan, and
then in the same way to Whitney. His gaze slides
into yours and it remains and it does not pass.
He pronounces your name. He said it. Your name. You.

You wipe your hands on the seat of your pants
and join the three others in front of the captain.

He crouches and signals for you to do the same
and his voice is like a thumbtack posting a bulletin.
"Listen, fellows. We're going to move up pretty damn soon.
We know that the Nips are planning a few surprises
and we've got to find out what the score is.
You men are a patrol. Sgt. Lindstrom is your leader.
Every company in the outfit is sending out similar units
so don't get trigger-happy or you might shoot your buddies.

"We need detailed preliminary reconnaissance of enemy positions and strong-
         points.
We've got to determine his capabilities as well as intentions—
how he can attack, where, when and in what strength.
Your mission will be to follow a general direction forward,
penetrating the Jap lines as far as you possibly can.
Locate gun casements, ammunition dumps, supply centers, and command posts.
Check deviations on compass readings. Indicate suitable routes of advance.
Get inside enemy areas. Find out his strength, his armament.
Ascertain his defiladed positions and the approximate degree of defilade.
Are there protective detachments in front or in the rear?
How far are they from the main body of troops?
What sort of soldiers are they? Young, old, careless, alert?
Can officers and noncoms be readily identified for sniper action?
Remember, men—we want facts and facts alone—not opinions."

He pauses. "Any questions?" There are none. "All right, then,
get ready to leave." He turns around and strides away.
Whitney is pleased. "I'm gonna get me a Jap!" He
elbows Lindstrom playfully in the stomach. "How about that, Sarge?"

"Make your reservation early. There won't be enough for everyone."

The latest fashion notes for the well dressed jungle scout
prescribe that the helmet be wound about with splotch cloth
so that it does not scrape loudly against overhanging twigs,
and that the stiff canvas leggins be unlaced and removed
to guard against noise caused by their brush against shrubbery.
The trouser cuffs are then wrapped tightly around the ankles
and are tucked into the sock tops to prevent snagging.

Anything that jangles must be muffled or left behind entirely.
The canteen cup is removed from the carrier and temporarily
set aside so the loosely fitting canteen will not rattle.
Dogtags are taped around the edges so they won't clink,
and beltbuckle, knife, buttons, bayonet, machete and all metal surfaces
that might attract enemy attention by glinting in the sunlight
are covered with a drab coating of rich mud.
Nothing white or out of harmony with jungle color schemes
must be visibly evident, and the face, neck and hands
are treated with a liberal application of G.I. blackface cream.

Lindstrom has moved down to confer with a supply sergeant
who has been able to set up shop, and he
draws two machetes and some grenades, and some chocolate bars,
ammo clips, mosquito repellant, sulfa powder and pills, jungle kits,
halazone tablets to purify water, and a vial of brandy.

Empty your pockets of all the things that might be
of value to the enemy in case you are captured,
and above all, don't take any letters you might have,
orders, sketches or any other bits of stray printed matter
which might give the Japs a clue to American strength
or the composition and identity of the units opposing them.

Take out your wallet and look at the random scraps
stuffed into the two leather compartments along its worn fold.
There are the souvenirs of your odd moments of memorabilia,
a pocket cemetery for the things you once thought important.

Here is the address of a girl living in Atlanta.
You met her at a party for soldiers and she
said you reminded her of her brother in the Navy
so she let you walk her home and kissed you.

Here is the key to the door of your house.
If ever you verged on idolatry, this bit of metal
was holy God and guardian angel and patron saint combined.
Don't look at it so long. Put it away quickly.

Here's a sales slip from a store selling military goods.
You did not find out that you had been overcharged
until the following morning, and you kept delaying your return
till you finally forgot what you wanted to complain about.

Here is one of those little ten cent store photographs
of an unregenerate brat you had a date with once,
and which you kept because the girl was undeniably photogenic.

Here's a calendar for the year of our war 1945,
printed in two colors and issued by the Moody Institute,
with various dates encircled for reasons long dead and buried.

Here's a receipt for a money order bearing number 13965
which you made out in the amount of six dollars
and sent on November tenth to someone you can't recall
for a purpose about which you haven't the slightest recollection.

Here are the words to a popular song, seasons old,
called "I'll Be Seeing You in All the Old Familiar
Places," which you copied out on a piece of paper
and wanted to memorize (but which you never did) because
you got sick and tired of merely humming the tune.

And here's a frayed, smudged item. It's your draft card.

23

There is a tide in the affairs of man, which,
taken between a blood test and an induction notice, leads
on to the Army. It's been a big adventure so
far. You've traveled and you've been around and you've seen
things and much has happened to you. But water is
wet whether it's off the shore of this island or
in Lake Michigan and mud is still dirty whether it's
on the banks of a jungle stream or near Claibourne,
Louisiana, and wherever you go you'll always find a placard
on a pine box saying, "Servicemen Admitted at No Charge."

Egan and Whitney are making their preparations and the rest
of the men glance at the three of you every
once in a while and you know that they are
wishing you luck. Sgt. Lindstrom has left the supply man
and is receiving last minute instructions from the company commander
and his back is turned toward you, hunched and intent.

Excitement is welling up inside of you and your mind
is recording a temperature and your thoughts are beginning to
wander and you are trying to follow them around. This
is the dark room in which your brain develops negatives
and imagination in verichrome presents a preview of nameless fears.
Why can't you take your personal bravery for granted and
not have to inquire after its health, but know that
when every moment becomes a crisis it will prove vigorous?
It's not the man in the fight that matters, but
the fight in the man, and even the Japs get
no medals for valor, since bravery is not considered exceptional.

You are curious about how Egan and Whitney feel and
you look at their faces but they are shielded by
deliberate cloakings of forced banter. Whitney is saying, "If it
wasn't for the money, I wouldn't take a job like
this." "Leave everything to Lindstrom," advises Egan. "He has a
difficulty for every solution." The other replies, "Well, I don't

know what I would do without him—but I'd rather!"
You join the conversation. "It takes all kinds of people
to make a world, but I sure wish those Japs
would go somewhere and make a world of their own."
"Yes," agrees Egan. "In spite of the fact that stocks
will go down, I'll be glad when the war's over
and I can go back home again." Whitney snorts, "Home?
What's home, mommy?" "There are just two things I would
do," continues Egan. "First, I'd strip my Garand and lay
it out on the porch to rust, and then I'd
sit and look at a woman till she came apart."

You smile and turn away. Good soldiers, both of them.
You wonder if the Japs aren't assembling similar patrols at
this very instant to penetrate the American beachhead, and if
they, too, aren't standing around waiting for the word to
proceed. Do you think they are kidding among themselves like
Egan and Whit? You doubt it. Somehow, discipline expresses itself
differently with men like these, and it is not the
actual fact of obedience that matters, but the willingness to
obey. Here, discipline arises from a consciousness of common aim
and from a pride before one's fellows and from a
shared understanding of the responsibilities involved. Sure, there's
still the spirit of "do as you're told and complain afterward," and
"take all the blame that can't be otherwise disposed of
and shut up about it." But behind it there is
the wisecrack and the democratic camaraderie of a winning team.

We're free men. They can't shoot us without our consent.

24

Sgt. Lindstrom is ready to start on the reconnaissance mission.
He waves his Tommy and says, "Come on, you guys,
let's go." You hastily pick up your rifle and join
the other three men in their diamond formation. Egan is
at the front point, while Lindstrom and Whitney will comprise
the flanks. You will maintain the rear position and serve
as getaway man. In the event of an enemy attack
you will detach yourself from the rest of the patrol
and attempt to carry important data back to the C.O.
You will also look toward the rear at frequent intervals
so as to give warning against a possible Japanese trap.

The sergeant removes his lensatic compass from its leather case.
He opens it and keeps it level in his palm.
He next allows the sensitive dial to come to rest
and then turns it slowly around until the luminous line
and the indicating arrow coincide. Then he compresses the damper
and sights the compass with a prominent object just ahead.
He takes the azimuth, an angle clockwise from magnetic North
to the point on which he happens to be sighting,
and moves off in a direction of seven degrees northwest,
which, allowing for magnetic declination, will be approximately due west.

Egan and Whitney have machetes, and they carry their pieces
slung. Lindstrom says, "We are patrol Red 21. The password
is 'Hallelujah,' and the countersign is 'You said it, brother.' "

There ahead of you is the jungle, looming and ominous.
This is the test. The books have been put away.
When you reach the perimeter defenses and pass beyond them,
Egan and Whitney will go forward alternately, covering each other
to the limit of visibility—probably about a dozen yards—
while Lindstrom will select the route and maintain the direction.
He carries a CE-11 lightweight, portable communications unit with a
sound-powered telephone slung around his neck, and the reel equipment
gripped in his left hand. The steel spool holds about

a quarter of a mile of assault wire which he
will lay along the jungle floor as he moves onward
and over which he will maintain contact with Captain MacDonald . . .

This way for a personally conducted tour of the community.
The shadowy dugout on your right is the Officers' Club,
where leaders by act of Congress take off their insignia
and work with the men in the anonymity of half-nakedness.

Over there is the amusement center, where a deluxe restaurant
is a dumped assortment of boxes and cases of rations,
a legshow is the rolled-up trouser cuffs of perspiring soldiers
and the penny palace is equipped with ultra-modern shooting galleries.

On your left are the department stores, open for business,
advertising clearance sales in drugs, hardware, fireworks and hunting equipment,
while pawnshops negotiate for collections of secondhand imported goods—
    unclaimed.

And nearer the beach, streets are being carefully laid out
for a quiet residential suburb, with homes of uniform construction—
each with a white wooden cross hanging above the door.

But not without amiable irony are the crudely lettered posters
that have cropped up outside of new foxholes and dugouts
which announce that "Through these portals pass the fastest mortals,"
or cheerfully caution the ignorant, bungling wayfarer against "Wet Paint."

And sticking out of nowhere are the inevitable little signposts
that title an imaginary boulevard, "Ocean Parkway" and inform you
that you have just turned the corner into "42nd Street"
and that Egan's size elevens have slogged into "Broadway," and
spattered you thoroughly from head to foot with "Times Square."

If you hurry, you might catch a subway express home.

25

The Lord is my shepherd; I shall not want (From
the beach you can hear the bulldozers, proud, pompous, snorting.
They view with cool disdain the obstructions of mere nature,
and are anxious to begin snuffling up dirt for corduroy
trails that engineers will build for the transport of supplies.)

He maketh me to lie down in green pastures (Here
is the vigilant sentry on guard at post number six.
The password is given and he motions you on, saying:
"Better crawl between here and the beginning of jungle growth.
If the Japs see you coming they'll wait in ambush."
You get down and proceed on your elbows and knees,
pushing aside the tall grass and scattering its shaken dust.
The stationary blocks of functionless air give way before you,
and the sunlight vibrates into jagged sparks of spurting shudders,
and greenness is peeled back to reveal its muddy rind
like the core of a rotten fruit the earth discarded.)

He leadeth me beside the still waters (You are passing
a sluggish stream hiding its brackish content under slimy plants,
and little whirlpools rise to the surface in floating bubbles.
Animals, lithe and robust, dive from their own established altitudes
down into the dank and the bleary shoal of murkiness
and splash about in the ebb of its tideless estuaries.)

He restoreth my soul (This is the time when greatness
in a man reveals its chemistry. You have no greatness
of your own, and if Lindstrom or Egan or Whitney
have none to spare, then borrow from those who have,
and offer your promissory note to a civilian named God.)

*He leadeth me in the paths of righteousness for His
name's sake* (The beginning of thick jungle land is reached
and the men straighten themselves up and move into it.
This is the place where heat and fire were born.
Before you came you didn't believe what others told you,

but now you can't believe the things you tell yourself.
The winding trail is a ragged ribbon of glue-mouthed mud
which varies in depth from your ankle to your knee.
The sound it makes is like a malicious child's prattle
as it leads an unsuspecting stranger on with nonsensical babbling,
and then, with a breathless giggle, it disappears from view.
But trails aren't safe anyhow, and Lindstrom gestures for the
group to begin hacking its way through the twisted undergrowth.)

Yea, though I walk through the valley of the shadow
of death (Here's where you cross the doormat of purgatory.
Your arms swing and your legs are raised and lowered,
but the rest of your body seems lost and insensate
to the thicket's keen talons and the earth's watchful summary
of your life's remaining footfalls. To die here and still
go to hell would be too damned hard to take.)

I will fear no evil for Thou art with me
(Lindstrom cautions, "Keep your eye on me, and if you
see me go down, it won't be from gravity, so
hit the dirt." He carries himself erect, like a battleflag,
and you know that he's worth his weight in cigarets.)

Thy rod and Thy staff, they comfort me (All you
can do is push ahead into the unknown, the jungle
primary, virgin and original, into the steaming and festering cavity
until your mind swoons and totters from its pendant cord
and your clothes hang from your bones in tattered shreds
and your skin gathers to itself all the assorted refuse
of ground and air and water and shrub and animal.)

Courage is fear singing a hymn arranged for four voices.

26

This is the locked and unused room of the world
about which the questions of the curious are politely ignored
and which, like its stock counterpart in a Hollywood scenario,
protects the family from having to witness its eugenic monstrosity.

Egan has not gone forward yet to his point position,
and Lindstrom stops the patrol in order to arrange signals.
He says, "One tap on the Tommy butt means halt.
Two taps mean danger, and three taps mean all clear.
If you see or hear anything suspicious, don't forget them
because in a spot like this we each have four
lives to worry about. Got it?" Whitney and Egan grunt
their agreement and you nod. "Okay, Egan, get up front."

Whitney moves to your left flank, about ten yards ahead,
and Lindstrom is to your right. Egan is rapidly disappearing
behind the heavy veil of frondescence. Now you are alone.

Wind up all the little alarm clocks of your mind.
Look around. No, you won't be able to see through
the jungle, but quite frequently you can look under it
because most of the vegetation is only a foot high
and there is a space between the undergrowth's high mark
and the lowest level reached by the crowded, overhanging vines.

Move as part of the ground. Be quick and silent.
Stretch out your toe exploringly while you keep the weight
of your body on your rear leg. You wish that
stealth was natural for you, but a lifetime of security
has made your movements deliberate and direct. Bright artificial lights
have reduced the efficiency of your vision, and all the
noise and din of city life has dulled your hearing.

But dammit, you've still got two ears on your head
and they were both approved by port of embarkation physicians
and they both stick out in the commonly accepted manner.

Can you distinguish the click of a rifle being loaded
from the sound of a twig being snapped in two?
Can you identify the fleeting thud of a human footstep
as against the pad of one of the jungle animals?
It is pitch, it is volume, it is tonal quality.
It is a patchwork of sounds, a complexity of loudnesses,
a momentary swish of audibility, a delicate flutter of frequencies.

Use your eyes, too. Sure, 'visibility limited' is an understatement
and maybe this is tobacco road on a dark night.
But at least you can see the indications of activity,
like broken stems of bushes or water spattered from leaves,
and you can avoid stepping on rotten logs and branches
and insecure footing and stones that are likely to roll.

Use your nose. The stink of defecation will tell you
whether or not Japs have been there and how recently.
Decomposition has a thin, sickish stench, and a dead Nip
left behind unburied may give you some very valuable clues.
Cigaret smoke persists for a long time in the jungle
and its odor may lead you directly to the enemy.
Then, too, you have been told that under field conditions
a Jap can be smelled from about ten feet away.

And use your head. Be alert, but take things easy.
Move with your muscles relaxed and save your body moisture.
Fear and exhaustion are the big dangers in jungle combat,
so don't get excited or panicky or lose your patience.
Still, don't get reckless and cocky. Make one tiny slip
and you might as well lie down and be buried.
Do it the hard way, the rough, tough, Army way.

Your class at college voted you Most Likely to Succeed.

27

They told you the jungle suit you're wearing is insectproof,
but won't somebody please come along and tell the insects?
Here in the rank growth, oblivious of their Latin nomenclature,
they welcome you with the zeal accorded fresh meat rations
and pass the happy news to friends, neighbors and relatives.

Waiting to use you as a filling station are elements
of all three divisions of tactical mosquitoes, with fighter escort,
the Anopheles, Aedes and Culex types, operating under unified command.
The Anopheles have wing markings, long feelers and fly silently,
coming in for landings with their bodies at 45 degrees
to the surface and biting with hind legs in the air.

The Aedes are identified by insignia of bands and lines,
usually of silver, white or yellow. They land and bite
with their bodies held parallel to the area of contact.

The Culex variety carry out raiding assignments and marauding missions.
The adults have no stripes on the chest or abdomen,
and their habits of attack are similar to the Aedes.
It will be of particular interest for you to note
that they don't care what you were in civilian life.

The ticks are present, too, with their flat, oval bodies
supported by from six to eight short and double-jointed legs.
They lurk on brush leaves, waiting for you to pass,
then attach themselves to clothing and ultimately to your skin.
They bury their heads under the epidermis and suck blood,
but remove themselves after they have enjoyed a hearty meal.

All manner of flies are zooming about. Small sand flies,
slender, two-winged, of light construction, but vicious on the assault,
as well as bloodsucking flies and the buffalo great flies
of which the female of the species is the deadlier.

Then there are the endless varieties of kissing or assassin bugs
with their dark brown bodies and their narrow, angular heads,
colonies of fleas, mandated gnats and whole republics of mites.

Leeches make getting next to your skin their one ambition,
and enter openings in your clothes—the fly, the collar,
and even the holes for laces in your jungle shoes.
They are perfectly at home anywhere, including up your rectum,
and when they bite they secrete a kind of juice
that lets them suck blood without fear of its clotting.

No doubt the fabulous little sweatbee is around here, too,
ready to foregather in mass meetings on any exposed parts
of your body and drink your perspiration so that they
may produce a form of inedible honey from your sweat.

There are large and hairy spiders with eight-inch leg spreads
that are relatively harmless, and there are little, unnoticeable spiders
that will strike without warning and hurt you like hell.

Under leaves, logs and stones are scorpions and land crabs
and centipedes dancing jigtime on their long rows of legs.
And hovering expectantly above them are chiggers and cone-nosed bugs
and an unlimited selection of airbone midges and flying bedbugs.
Ants are everywhere. Large, small, medium—red, black and white.
Some bite and some sting and some bite and sting.
The biting ones overwhelm their victims by attacking in swarms
while the stinging ones confine their maneuvers to sporadic infiltrations
and pour their formic acid into openings in the skin.

And then there is the universally uninvited parasite, the louse.
It is small, gray, wingless, with claws on its legs.
Once it deposits itself in the seams of your clothing
it will be almost impossible for you to remove it
and you will go right on getting lousier and lousier.

All the insects seem to sting with a Japanese accent.

28

When I consider Thy heavens, the work of Thy fingers,
the moon and the stars which Thou hast ordained, what
is man that Thou art mindful of him? (You are
going through the jungle and you see that there are
no paved sidewalks or curbstones or sewer gratings or automobiles
and there is nothing for the comfort and convenience of
creatures such as you. Everything here and elsewhere on earth
was made for the perpetuation of animals—dull, physical animals—
and this means animals eating and animals sleeping and animals
giving birth to more animals. The chicken was intended to
eat and be eaten, not by men but by animals,
and there is nothing in nature's cookbook that says it
is supposed to be roasted and served with browned potatoes
and stuffed with sliced apples and put on a dish.)

For Thou hast made him a little lower than the
angels and has crowned him with glory and honor (Everything
men have done to improve themselves has been a perversion
of original purpose. They have made buildings out of dust.
They have made apparel from a sheep's coat of hair.
They have chopped down trees and inscribed their histories thereon.
And all that they have accomplished has been the product
of an accidental intellect for which God was not responsible
because His work was finished with creation. Jungle law was
the only legislation laid down in the beginning, and that
is the root they will stumble over in the end.)

The lines are fallen unto me in pleasant places (So
here is your inheritance, your legacy, your residue of gain
after deductions have been made under jungle law. By continued
exposure to insects you may manage to contract malaria, filariasis,
yellow fever, dengue fever, relapsing fever, pappataci, espundia, oriental sore,
typhus, trench fever, bubonic plague, tularemia, dumdum fever or loa-loa.

If your supply of drinking water happens to become contaminated,
you may look forward with confidence to an impending attack
of dysentery, cholera, typhoid fever, helminthic infection or undulant fever.

If you expose yourself to the fungi of the locale
you may be host to the pigmented patches of skin
that characterize pinta, besides finding trichosporosis thriving in your hair,
dhobie itch spread wherever you find it difficult to scratch
and athlete's foot festering in the spaces between your toes.)

Yea, I have a goodly heritage (The thorns and spines
of poisonous or irritant trees and vines and shrubs and
miscellaneous plants may cause severe blisters. The sap of the
Beach Apple and the Mango tree will occasion painful rashes
and sores which heal with difficulty, while the nuts of
the Kaong, Dumayaka and Fishtail palms are covered with needles
which penetrate and irritate the skin. The Nipai, a twining
vine, produces a wrinkled pod which is armed with stiff
barbs that pierce the clothing, and if you come across
some large purple flowers that exude the odor of decaying
meat, it's the pungapung plant, whose stalk emits poisonous juices.)

Therefore my heart is glad and my glory rejoiceth (Pain
and swelling may result from careless exposure to the dry,
black gum of the Ligas tree, while the milky white
sap of the Buta-buta causes serious inflammation and total blindness.
If the oil of the Kamanday tree enters your body
it will almost certainly prove fatal, as will the bark
of the Abuab tree and the sap of the Dalit.
In addition, you may encounter coral snakes, moccasins and vipers
as well as wild hogs, bats, alligators and swamp lizards.)

But your greatest danger is from your fellow human beings.

29

You brush through space even too small for a shadow,
and the stultifying air is like a repressive suction cup
drawing the strength slowly out of your mind and body.
Your guts feel like they're clouding up for a storm
and the sweat dribbles from your pores in freeflowing streamlets.

This climate increases your concentration of blood plasma and urine,
and any undue exertion will send your body temperature soaring.
Don't let your perspiration roll off. It helps cool you
by means of evaporation, so smear it over your skin . . .

O Lord High Potentates of the Smithsonian Institution, and Division
of Wildlife Management of the United States Department of Agriculture,
whoever told you the jungle wasn't hotter than Washington, D. C.?

What if you're lost or cut off from your unit
and have to spend the night here, or even days?
Will you be able to survive with no prepared food
and your water used up, and all your frail inadequacies
constantly pursuing you in thoughts that refuse to remain unthinkable?

Shoes will rot out, clothes will become ragged and filthy.
Legs will be covered with jungle sores, bodies will become
lean and hard, faces will grow thin, furtive and lupine.
All the locks and hasps and destination tags and stickers
of these few stray and unidentified items of human baggage
will come loose, and covers will corrode on their hinges
and fall off and spill the miserable contents all out.

Dammit, stop going around with your mind in a sling.
Jungle hardships are just a myth. Why, it's perfectly possible
to live here indefinitely if you don't lose your head.
Your individual medical jungle kit contains a rubber-lined food bag,
an ounce bottle of Fraser's solution, 200 water purifying tablets,
a package of sulfadiazine pills and bottles of quinine sulphate,
adhesive tape, bandages, aspirin and a can of foot powder.

You also have insect repellent and a change of socks.
What else do you want—an egg in your beer?

Watch the monkeys, and if you see them eating anything,
you can eat it too. Besides, they are edible themselves.
In fact, almost all the animals and birds and reptiles
you will run into may be classed as high-priority rations.
Wild hog and wild duck and wild pigeon, flying fox,
fish, eels—all can be eaten, along with toasted termites,
grilled grasshoppers and baked beetle grubs. Fresh fruit in season
is also available, and you may find bananas, oranges, lemons,
breadfruit, wild raspberries, nakarika, papaya, mangoes, hogplum and star appl
while among vegetables the jungle menu offers a choice of
taro, yam, manioc, palm cabbage, hearts of pandamus and rattan.

The winelist, of course, is limited due to wartime shortages,
but you may enjoy natural fruit juices or coconut milk.
Water may be readily secured, although purification will be necessary.
You can sterilize it by boiling for about five minutes,
but if you can't do so, treat with halazone tablets.

Rain is regular, and conforms to a fairly predictable timetable
and rocky pockets or crevices will frequently hold a pool.
Birds fly toward water, trails often will lead to water,
and for the most part you will find it downhill.
Many plants have water stored in their stems and leaves,
and you may quench your thirst by chewing on them.
Also, the fluid content in the stomachs of wild animals
is quite safe and nutritious in spite of its taste.

Sure, there's food here, exotic and palatable, and there's water
and no doubt you could make yourself a real banquet.

Still, you'd rather have it at an American Legion convention.

30

The jungle growth is becoming too heavy for adequate visibility.
Every minute it gets thicker, and now it's like tomorrow.
Lindstrom signals for the patrol to abandon its diamond formation
and reform behind him at close intervals in single column.
He unslings his Tommy gun and carries it at port,
while behind him moves Egan, observing ground to the right,
followed by Whitney who covers the area on his left.
You maintain your position in the rear, frequently looking back.

Give careful scrutiny to terrain that might offer tactical possibilities.
Watch out for newly barked roots or a broken twig
or bent grass or scuffed tree trunks or malformed branches.
If you find anything that might indicate the enemy's presence,
tap twice on your rifle stock to warn your buddies
to break the file and get set for all-around defense.

Don't expect to see a Jap unless, by accident, you
bump into one face to face. He's too well hidden.
And don't think you'll hear anything, either. All jungle noises
are confined, as though they are from inside of a
bottle. Sounds travel slowly, and the crack of his rifle
will reach you only after the bullet has struck home.

He knows you're coming. He's waiting for you out there.
He's an expert in counterpatrolling and skilled in preparing ambushes.
He's got an instinct for camouflage, and patience and trigger-discipline
and he'll wait all day, if necessary, up to his
waist in swamp slime for a single shot at you.
He's counting on you to underestimate his toughness and spirit
and the quality of his weapons and accuracy of fire,
and he wants you to think he's stupid as hell
when all the time he's a resourceful, wily little bastard
who knows more about you than you know about him.

His command of English is considerably better than your knowledge
of Japanese, and he has been schooled in Phrases for

Combat, learning such useful military deceptions as "This way, fellows,"
"Don't shoot, pal, it's me," "Hey, buddy—got a smoke?"
"Help, I'm wounded!"—all with the accent on hot lead
and conjugation into past tense of the verb, to be.

His physical conditioning and battle hardening began in early youth.
Obstacle courses, wall scaling, extended drill, swimming and double-time marching
kept him in trim, while judo, bayonet practice and fencing
produced a sharp fighting edge. The military phases of education
were preferably carried out under the most adverse weather conditions
and simulated actual battle problems as realistically as circumstances permitted
while officers kept him on the move around the clock
on the assumption that he already knew how to sleep
and that he needed training in how to stay awake.

Don't figure him to give you any breaks. He won't.
It's hard for you to realize that someone hates you,
but if that someone is anywhere, you'll find him here.
Before being detailed to active duty in the Pacific theatre,
he served a period of indoctrination in China, and the
smell and the sight and the feel of battered torsos
are nothing new to him. He kills with reflex action
and he does it dirtily, viciously, with no quarter given.

You can rely on him to fight to the last.
And remember. He's tough and tricky and sneaky and treacherous.
He shows a sacrificial devotion to duty, and he says,
"If my arms are broken I will kick my enemy.
If my legs are injured, then I will bite him.
If my teeth loosen, I will glare him to death!"

But right now he's just as scared as you are.

31

Egan has stopped. Whitney has stopped. They both crouch tensely.
You pause with your body stiffly tangent to the universe.
You cannot see Lindstrom, but you hear him tap once,
then again, on the wooden stock of his Tommy gun.

Stand still. Be quiet. If you're surrounded, the noise you
would make getting flat on your middle would be like
taking your finger out of a hole in the dike
of enemy firepower. You're better off remaining on your feet.
The tall brush breaks up your silhouette, and you can
move more quickly in any direction. Listen. Listen very carefully.
You can hear the molecules in the air marching past
to the threshing and hammering drum beat of your pulse.

Turn your head and look behind you. Can you see
anything? Only mud and vines and scrub and a fly
buzzing in lazy loops and trees leaning on their years
and a single leaf falling like a drop of eternity.

A shadow darkens your awareness. You twist around, facing forward.
There's Lindstrom. His hand is lifted. He whispers, "Stay here,
you guys. There's something rotten out front and I'm saving
myself a trip to Denmark." He sidles out of your
vision and the rustling curtain of foliage swings shut again.

You feel the jungle weaving you into its green tapestry.
"Stay here . . ." Okay. You'll stay. You'll stay because there's nothing
else to do, and you'll stay here because there's nowhere
else to do it. The whole thing is like a
poorly written play, full of dramatic build-ups that never reach
a climax and climaxes that are never built up to.
And there's no showmanship or staging or colorful lighting effects
and the characters are plain, ordinary dopes, and the lines
said and the gestures made are plain, ordinary and dopy.
It's stupid and uninspired and insulting to the simple dignity
of human beings . . . But it is having a record run

and people come from all over and they call it
the Big Show and they will go on doing it
until maybe someday there will be a special performance given
and no one will attend. Then the empty theatre will
crumble and souvenir hunters will take home parts of it
and say, "Look, here is a little piece of war,"
and people will laugh because it is just a handful
of plain, ordinary dopy dust, and not a mangled body.

Egan and Whitney are poised motionlessly, like trained bird dogs,
while silence stretches out like a tightly drawn rubber sheet.
Now they stir anxiously as a cautious footstep is heard
and rifles are raised in readiness. Lindstrom's low voice reassures,
"It's me, fellows," and he creases the brush and reappears.
He puts his hand on Whitney's shoulder and beckons Egan
and you over to him, and you see excitement in
his eyes. "Listen," he says, "I saw a T-shaped limb
that looked unnatural to me, and damned if it didn't
turn out to be a rest for field glasses. There's
a Jap observation post right behind it hidden from view
by grass, moss and stones. At first I thought it
was abandoned, and I was just getting set to investigate
when I saw a sentry standing guard. Lucky his back
was toward me, or he would have given the alarm.
Now, here's the deal. We can't bypass him because of
the stream on our right, so we'll do a quiet
disposal job. We will attract his attention from the front
while someone sneaks behind and knifes him from the rear."

Patriotism means allowing the enemy to die for his country.

32

Egan says, "I'll do it, Sarge." Whitney mutters, "Hell no,
send me!" Lindstrom shakes his head. "Neither of you are
going." His mouth is grim. "Today I am a man."

He takes his Tommy gun from his shoulder and unhooks
the reel, handing both to you. Then he whispers, "You
boys cut across to your left for about fifteen yards.
That should put you directly in front of the sentry.
Meanwhile, I'll be skirting around to his rear and getting
into position for our little squeeze play." He looks down
at his watch. "Check the time." You bring your wrist
up to your face and stare at the white roundness
of the dial strapped to your skin and at the
pale green of the figures around its edge and at
the two webbed hands pointing impersonally and at the jerky
sweep of the longer, thinner second hand moving around them.
"I've got 0631," Lindstrom announces. "What have you got?" Egan
murmurs agreement while Whitney makes a slight adjustment. You nod.
"Give me a minute or so to get set," he
resumes, "and at 0633 do something to stimulate his curiosity.
Make animal noises or wave a branch back and forth.
But don't worry. Before he has a chance to fire
I'll be quietly at work with my handy little tool.
Okay, now—let's go!" He moves off as he came.

The three of you are alone, and you gaze at
each other for a brief moment and then turn sideways
in the indicated direction. Whitney is ahead and softly counts
the number of wary steps he takes, while you are
directly behind him, and are followed by Egan. Easy now.
A stumble, a slip of shoe leather on a root,
a fall or even an effort to regain your balance
will draw a shot and some highly unwelcome Japanese curiosity
and the whole mission will blow up in your face.

Anyhow, you're glad Lindstrom didn't ask you to do it.
You killed a man. Sure. But all you had to

do was squeeze a trigger and all you could feel
was the slap of the rifle butt in your armpit,
and all you had to look at was an alien
figure fifty feet away grow instantly rigid and drift downward
in the strange languor of lifelessness. But this is different.
You'd have to feel flesh under your fingers and hear
the point of your knife scrape against some internal bone
and see the last paroxysm tremble on the fulminating skin.

Whitney stops. He parts a few blades of tall grass
and peers through. Then, with his arm low and palm
distended, he motions toward the ground. You lower your body
and rest on your elbows. Egan joins you noiselessly and
Whitney lets himself down so that you all lie parallel.
He breathes, "He's coming this way. Keep watching straight ahead
and you'll be able to see him cross our path."

You look between the stalks of brush cane and bamboo,
and you think to yourself, "Little brown brother, we are
about to separate you from your place in the sun.
The spirit of Bushido has been spoken of from olden
times in these words: 'Among flowers the cherry, among men
the warrior.' We do not suppose that death will change
your point of view, but it will effectively end it,
and when your futile existence has been finalized, death will
despise you because you have chosen to live despising life.
Little brown brother, it is God's will that you die.

"We will do our best to collaborate with the Almighty."

33

Through the corners of your eyes you see the Jap
sentry approaching. He traverses your line of sight and as
his searching scrutiny passes over your hiding place, you instinctively
draw back and try to make yourself small and inconspicuous.

The Nip is wearing remnants of a worn khaki shirt
and you can see that he carries around his neck
an amulet in the form of a small cloth bag
which probably contains some earth from his native village shrine
and which he firmly believes will protect him in battle.
He has on his split-toed tabi and puttees wound sloppily
up to his bare knees. Around his waist is a
"fundashi" or loin cloth, with a pocket on its side
out of which protrudes a knife handle. Across his shoulder
is a bandolier of ammunition, while carried in his hands
is his rifle with its gleaming bayonet attached. Jauntily cocked
on his head is a steel helmet camouflaged with foliage.

The tour of his post ends where the slight rise
on which the observation station has been situated descends to
the marshy level of the stream's approaches, and the sentry
turns to walk back. "Little brown brother . . . little brown brother,
you are the customer listed on our bill of lading.

"You're just a runt, barely more than five feet tall,
and you're galled at the fact that the white man
is bigger than you are, and it spurs you on
to work twice as hard for longer lengths of time.
During your occupation of this island, you rose before morning
and, after a brief toilet, you began your daily worship
with meditation and a respectful reading of the Imperial mandate.

"You'll labor from pain at dawn to groan at night,
and spend the rest of your time fighting or marching.
And you'll do it all on a handful of rice
and maybe a few scraps of dried fish or some

chopped seaweed or sliced ginger or gourd shavings washed down
with sake or a beverage made from Mamushi snake flesh.
And even without food or drink you can keep going
for a long period, and at meal times you will
pretend that you have eaten and contentedly display a toothpick.

"There are two chances in three that in civilian life
you were either a farmer or an urban factory worker,
and when you write home you are permitted to say:
'I fight south of the equator and need more competition.
The enemy is weak. I fight fiercely and I live
under conditions very similar to those of the regular residents.'"

Here he comes again. "Little brown brother, when your relatives
receive the official notification of your heroic death in action,
they will rigidly abstain from eating fish for 49 days
in mourning. You will never sit among them and exaggerate."

He pivots and retraces his steps. With sudden apprehension you
see that he has paused and is looking at the
pile of loose stones. Could he have detected Lindstrom's presence?
No. His attitude is expectant rather than suspicious. It occurs
to you that he might be waiting for a relief.
Jesus Christ, we'll have to work fast. We'll have to
get him out of the way in a hurry and
set a trap for the next one. Where is Lindstrom?

The sentry resumes his walk. Egan's hand grips your arm.
You see a slight tremor in the bushes opposite you.
It's Lindstrom. His knife is unsheathed. The Jap's back is
angled half toward him. This will be quick and clean.

Japs don't mind death. It's a nice change from living.

You look at your watch. "Now!" you whisper, "Now!" Whitney takes hold of a slender bamboo stalk and shakes it and the noise seems like a clap of piercing thunder. The Jap whirls at the sound and instantly leaps to a position of readiness, with legs spread wide and rifle thrust out sideways as though to stand off an attack. You see Lindstrom reach out with his left hand and pick up a fistful of dirt which he will probably use to throw in the Nip's eyes if he should happen to turn around accidentally. He starts forward, slowly at first, hoping to get within striking distance before being discovered.

Your breath is smothered with tension. He takes one step, then another. Five or six more and he'll be able to leap on the enemy and dig his trench knife into the sentry's back. Stealthily he is narrowing the gap.

Suddenly, there is a crash of brittle underbrush behind him and your head jerks at the sound and you see another Jap running out from behind the rock pile, heading straight for Lindstrom with his rifle distended and his bayonet held high for a jab at the throat. The sentry in the foreground wheels around and is momentarily stupefied at the situation. Then he, too, raises his piece and charges.

Quick! Get on your feet! Smash through the restraining barrier of brush. You see a look of consternation on Lindstrom's face. He is standing there with his knife frozen in his hand. You are free of the tangled vines now and the butt of the Tommy gun is pressed against your ribs. The first Jap reaches him and lunges with a short, upward stab. Lindstrom sidesteps, throws the dirt in his face and with the same motion grabs hold of the rifle barrel. His other hand is raised to drive the knife into the Nip's exposed body, but the sentry closes in to aid his comrade and parries the blow,

catching the blade in a hook near the hilt of
his bayonet. You can't shoot now! You can't! You're sure
to hit your own man. Whitney and Egan are up.
Let's get 'em! Let's get 'em! Let's get 'em with
our knives or bayonets or bare hands. Let's get 'em!

You throw aside the submachine gun and run for the
struggling group, drawing your knife from its sheath at your
hip. Lindstrom has lost his footing and falls to the
earth. The knife is sprung from his hand and slithers
crazily along the ground. The Jap standing over him is
drawn back for a stroke. You jump with your fingers
outstretched and catch the front part of his throat, jerking
his head back. You can feel the muscles in his
neck convulsing and you can see the look of surprise
and immediate terror in his eyes. You twist the knife
into his back, putting all your strength behind its penetration.

You feel his gasping breath on your wrist and it
is mixed with saliva and the rifle drops from his
hands and blood bursts from his mouth and trickles down
his chin and he shivers. Then all at once he
becomes limp and you know he is dead. You withdraw
your stained knife and lower the carcass to the grass.

Egan and Whitney have already felled the other enemy soldier
and he lies with his knees retracted to his stomach
and his eyes bulging and sightless and his bony hands
pressed to the Imperial seal engraved on his rifle receiver.

They closed his life's book and sat on the cover.

35

Lindstrom is lying on the ground in great pain, his
shirt beginning to show bright red from a bayonet wound
in the midsection. He swallows his agony but his mouth
lets a little of it out every time he breathes.

Egan forces him to take some sulfa pills and loosens
his belt so that the wound is exposed. Lindstrom is
fully conscious and smiles wanly and says, "Looks like I've
sprung a leak!" Whitney asks, "How does it feel, Sarge?"
and Lindstrom's eyes cloud over and his voice becomes thick
and slow. "Like I've been—eating—too many—green apples."
His lips work for a moment and his eyes close
and he passes out with a little sigh of leftover
breath. Egan applies the compress from his first aid pouch
to the gash, wraps it around his waist and ties
the bandage securely at the hip. You say, "We've got
to get him away from here. This place is practically
Tokyo Boulevard." There has been no outcry, no alarm, but
you are afraid that the observation post might be a
rendezvous point for Jap counterpatrols. "Let's lift him up and
carry him over to less open ground." Whitney takes hold
of his shoulders underneath the arms and you lift up
his ankles, while Egan prevents his back from sagging downward
by bracing Lindstrom's body with his arms held stiffly outward.

You were second in command. Now you're in full charge.
You will make the decisions and carry the responsibility for
the success of the mission. The other two men will
look to you for leadership, and if you have it
they will follow you. Don't let them see how Lindstrom's
wound has affected you, don't let them see how frightened
and insecure you feel. No, you can't fool them into
believing that coolness and presence of mind is something that
you sew on with a corporal's stripes, but if you
show hesitancy or confusion you'll lose control. Be sure of
yourself, be calm, confident. Put on an act, a front.

You pause where the vegetation becomes more matted and tangled.
"Here's a good place. Let's put him down. Easy now."
You lower the feet first, and Egan and Whitney go
to their knees in order to let him down without
jarring him unduly. The blood has been drained from his
head and his face is white. The gauze pad is
a darkening expansion of redness. You add, "One of us
will have to take him back to the command post
for medical attention. How about it, Whit? Think you can
handle him?" He replies, "Sure. He'd do the same for
me, wouldn't he?" "Okay, then. In a minute or so
the bleeding will stop and then we'll hitch him to
your back. Meanwhile, Egan and I will hide those two
dead Japs out there and recover our weapons." You beckon
to Egan and turn back to the clearing once again.

There are the Nips, dirty and repulsive, even in death.
You straddle one of them and stoop down and lift
it to your shoulder while Egan hoists the other. You
walk a few paces and lay the body down in
a patch of tall grass which conceals it from view . . .
"In serving on the seas, be a corpse that is
saturated with water. In serving on land be a corpse
that is covered with weeds. In serving in the sky
be a corpse that challenges clouds. Let us all die
close by the side of our Emperor with no regrets."

War is a Japanese industry. And these are the unemployed.

36

You step over to the point where you had discarded
Sgt. Lindstrom's Tommy gun, and you retrieve it. Then you
part the slim stalks of brush cane in search of
your rifle. You see it partially covered by bent grass
where you had lain it down and you pick it
up and sling it on your shoulder. The reel of
telephone wire is also on the ground, and you lift
it with your free hand and tug the unwound strand
loose from the snatching fingers of burr and of nettle.

Egan has recovered the two Japanese rifles which had been
lying where their owners had fallen, and he holds one
of them in each hand. He asks, "What in hell
are we going to do with these?" You say, "Well,
maybe we can use them as splints to give Lindy
more support while he's being carried back to the company
area. Lucky it isn't very far. Only about sixty yards."

He is grasping the weapons by their barrels at a
point a little below the hilt of the bayonet and
you move closer to examine them. They seem to be
a much later model than the old 38th Year and
they have some sort of a mount which can be
folded forward to catch on the stock when it is
not in use. There is a device on the end
of the muzzle which apparently is designed to hide flashes,
but you are mostly interested in the rubberized fabric slings
attached to swivels on the stock, which you see can
be readily removed in order to strap the pieces securely
in place to hold the injured man's sides more firmly.

You make your way back to the casualty, gingerly skirting
a clump of thorny barbs, with Egan following behind you.
In the emergency you have become incautious, and now you
look searchingly at the approaches to the observation post, lest
the sounds of rapid movement and struggle attracted enemy attention.

Whitney is leaning over Sgt. Lindstrom, who is moaning semi-consciously
and turning his head slowly from one side to another.
Whitney whispers, "I think he's coming to." You drop the
Tommy gun and the reel and rest on one knee.
You say, "We'll have to make it PDQ and try
to get him comfortably trussed up before he snaps out
of it. Use the slings on these Jap rifles to
hold the braces in position and tear up a piece
of his uniform to bind them, if necessary. Meanwhile, I'll
make contact with Captain MacDonald over the telephone and ask
him to have a couple of medics with a stretcher
stand by." You grip the canvas harness of the phone
which Lindstrom had borne across his shoulders, and which has
now slipped within his bent forearm. Egan assists you in
removing the mouthpiece and earphone attachments from around his neck.

Whitney takes out the magazine from each of the Jap
rifles and spills the bullets on the ground and covers
them with loose dirt. Then he removes bayonets and prepares
to adjust the guns with their barrels along Lindstrom's legs.

You struggle into the straps of the telephone set, letting
the mouthpiece dangle just below your left shoulder and adjusting
the lightweight reel against your hip so that it will
unwind freely and trail its strand when you move on.
You take the test clips of the handset cord and
connect them to the spool terminals and you hear the
buzz and gurgle of electrical wires in contact with others.

Steady your voice. You are about to impersonate a soldier.

37

The end of the line is probably hitched to a
magnetic phone and you'll have to monitor before you can
get through. Don't raise your voice. Speak softly. "Captain MacDonald,
Red 21 . . . Red 21 calling Captain MacDonald". . . You pause for
a second, waiting. There is a click and you recognize
the captain's voice. "Red 21. This is headquarters, E Company.
I've been parked on my ass here, sweating you out.
Why in hell haven't you been keeping me informed on
what gives?" You identify yourself. "We had a little argument
with two Japs we encountered at an enemy observation post.
Sgt. Lindstrom is a casualty, with a bayonet wound in
the stomach. Whitney is going to bring him back in.
Can you have him met with a couple of corpsmen
and some whole blood? Just have them follow the telephone
wire." He says, "Lindstrom? Jesus, that's bad." His speech withdraws
as though he had removed his mouth from the transmitter
in order to give instructions to a waiting orderly, then
it comes back strongly, "Okay. What is your present position?"
You answer, "We started out at 270 azimuth and can't
be more than about five minutes away from the outer
perimeter. Whitney is almost ready to start, and Egan and
I are pushing on to complete the mission." He replies,
"Good. I'll hold on at this end for anything you
are able to report. Tell me everything you see or
hear." You affirm, "Will do." He clicks off. You disconnect.

Whitney and Egan have partially succeeded in trussing Lindstrom up.
He lies quietly, and his movements are weak and spasmodic.
You say, "The medics will meet him with blood." Your
eyes focus on the soaked bandage. "Lord knows he needs
a change of oil." Whitney urges, "You guys take off.
I can handle him by myself." You ask, "Are you
sure, Whit?" He doesn't look up. "Sure I'm sure, Goddamit!"

You remove Lindstrom's lensatic compass and you fasten it onto
your own belt. Then you pick up the Tommy gun

and prepare to move. Egan is on his feet, with
his rifle in his hands. He says, "So long, Whit,"
and Whitney answers, "So long." Then you say, "So long,"
and Whitney lifts up his arm and replies, "So long."

The two of you turn and direct your bodies into
the jungle, with you leading and Egan following closely behind.
"So long . . . So long." That's all there is to it,
Egan and Whitney and you saying So long to each
other when all the time you're really talking to the
guy on the ground. "So long . . . So long." Nobody gets
a cork in his throat and nobody tries to play
hero, because the feeling of a man for a man
is one of those shining jewels that custom decrees must
be worn inconspicuously. He'll get the lavender gizzard for this
and maybe the DSC and he'll tell everybody that he
got his medals for doing what he intended doing anyhow.

You feel that Egan is looking at you and that
his eyes are asking, Now what? You wish you had
a more detailed map of the island, but your mouth
curls when you think of a flat piece of paper
with lines and numbers on it to indicate elevations and
some pretty green coloring to represent jungle. Forward, go forward.
Slip on the wet gorse and fall blindly into mud
and stagger free of roots and vines and trip over
thorny entanglements and stumble and pitch and lurch and totter.

Chaos created this lump of clay in its own image.

38

You hook up the telephone set once more for contact
with Captain MacDonald. You hear his voice at the other
end of the wire. You say, "We are moving out
again, still about 25 yards in from the left bank
of the stream.". . ."How's the terrain?". . ."It's pretty rugged, but
the vegetation isn't quite as dense as it was before.
We're going up a slight incline and the ground seems
to be a little more firm.". . ."What do you see?". . .
"There are a couple of trees directly ahead that have
had their tops sliced off, and splinters are all over
the place. I believe we're entering the area that the
Navy must have shelled before the initial landings were made."

You move along and are briefly exposed to sunlight, casting
a shadow from which you draw back in momentary fear.
Well, it makes good sense to be afraid right now,
and you're glad that your reflexes are lean and hard
and functional, with no fat to them. It's a big
poker game, and you're playing your cards close to your
chest and watching the dealer carefully and betting your strength.

Other men have walked like this. Other Americans have driven
their bodies through long black minutes that shrouded their minds
and dropped in deep folds over their hearts. And theirs
was a shadow they could not escape but which bobbed
crookedly in the relentless gray dust of a scorched road.

Out of Bataan they marched, to San Fernando in Pampanga province,
with their grinning captors beating them with sticks and herding
them through blistering heat without rest or food or water.
Occasionally they were forced to go very fast, with the
Japs pacing them on bicycles, and at other times they
were held down to a slow agonized shuffle. Some threw
themselves moaning beside the highway, but the strong were not
permitted to help the weak and had to turn away
and wait for the shots that they knew would come.

At night they were placed in a cramped bullpen and
given a messkit of badly cooked rice, while during their
hours of slumber the Jap guards amused themselves by charging
into the enclosure from time to time with bayonets fixed.

From San Fernando they were freighted to Capiz Tarlac in small
boxcars with the doors locked. Many of the prisoners were
suffering from diarrhea and dysentery and could not control themselves
so that the horrible stench became alloyed with the heat
and hung from their bodies like a mass of chains.

For months they were retained at Camp O'Donnell, where they
lived among filth and maggots and stood in line for
ten hours to get a drink of water and couldn't
summon strength enough to dig graves for their departed buddies.
American flags were habitually and designedly used as rags in
the Jap kitchens, and rations included rice, with an intermittent
bit of potato and a few mango beans over a
period of several weeks and a spoonful of coconut lard.

Later they were moved to Cabanatuan Concentration Camp in Luzon,
and when several tried to escape from this new hell,
they were cruelly flogged about the feet and the legs
until they could no longer stand up on them but
had to fall, and then were kicked and jumped upon.
Next they were stripped of their ragged clothing and tied
with ropes and propped up to endure the ravaging blaze
of the sun for two full days, after which they
were taken down and ceremoniously beheaded before their assembled comrades

Do unto Japs as Japs do unto you—but first.

39

You talk into the telephone. "This area is pretty well pockmarked with shell holes, Captain, and outside of some vines hung between trees to form entanglements, I can't see any signs of obstacles or fortifications. Just craters and dirt piles." . . . "Did you say dirt piles?" . . . "Yes, it looks as though they made some effort to bury their dead before withdrawing." . . "Dead, hell! Those pits probably contain guns and ammo that they planted there during the bombardment. If we occupy the position they'll sneak out at night, dig up the stuff and use it on us. Find out what's underneath them."

You wave to Egan and approach one of the mounds. The loosely packed earth readily gives way before your shoes and your foot strikes a hard, metal substance. It is a sheet of heavy galvanized iron, about three feet square. You take hold of a corner of it and lift it up so that it tilts backward, shedding the sand.

"You're right, Captain. One of the piles is really the entrance to a dugout and it has a machine gun in it all set for use." . . . "Okay. Replace the dirt and keep moving." . . . You put back the covering and shove some earth on top of it before turning to go.

Directly ahead is a patch of growth about waist high and you stoop low so that your head is not exposed against a lighter background. You wonder if you have been seen, if some sniper is waiting for you to emerge into the open, if your movements are being watched. Observe from depressions, not from elevations. Here's a little ravine. Follow it along, and keep in defilade. Don't look over rocks, bushes, tree trunks, but peep out from the side, the shady side, or through cracks or holes or openings.

You stop. Through the brush you can see some shrubbery shaking, a short distance away. Egan has seen it, too

and gets down quickly. You are seized with sudden alarm.
Is this the finish? An ambush? A trap? You flatten.
Captain MacDonald's voice is coming over the phone. "Red 21,
hello, hello. What's been going on? Can you hear me?"

Your throat is tied in a knot. You say, "They're
coming, they're coming." You see the flash of machete blades,
and the sound of excited jabbering reaches your ears. You
are relieved. They wouldn't be making so much noise if
they knew that two Americans were within a stone's throw
You hollow your hands over your mouth. "It's just a
clearing unit. There are seven men and a noncom. They
have sickles, axes, oil cans and marking materials. One of
them carries a sketchboard with a map apparently on it,
and he's making reference notes. They are coming this way
but I'm sure they haven't seen us because they're talking
and laughing. Behind them are two single files of soldiers,
one on each side of the trail, with five paces
between men. They carry rifles, and they have bits of
foliage stuck on their helmets and in the pockets and
buttonholes of their uniforms. Some of them carry nets over
their heads, with palm leaves laced into them for camouflage. . . ."
"How many would you say there were?" . . . "I don't know,
they're still coming. They might be several companies strong. Here
comes a squad armed with grenade dischargers. There is a
microphone patrol and a wire cutting team, and details with
D-handle shovels are deploying to repair the damage to the
fortifications. Good lord, the little sons of bitches are everywhere!" . . .

They are paid to kill. And they need the money.

40

"The approach march is being made with platoons intervaled at
two yards, with a squad on each side to protect
the flanks. Contact is maintained by connecting files and runners.
I can't distinguish any officers by their battledress, although there
are quite a few boys giving orders. This place is
certainly filling up. Here comes a medical detachment with a
casualty transport platoon, carrying rolled-up stretchers, and behind them is
a group of supply men with boxes of shells." . . . "Shells?
Are there any cannon present?" . . . "No, Captain, that's what I
can't understand, unless they're smoke shells." . . . "Yes, they probably are.
They'll fire them from knee mortars when they retreat or
change position. What other armament do you see?" . . . "Only small
arms and automatic weapons. Rifles, light and heavy machine guns,
grenade dischargers, mortars and Tommy guns. Riflemen predominate, and each
carries three leather boxes of ammo attached to his belt." . . .
"Would you say that their intentions were defensive, then?" . . . "From
what I am able to observe, I would say that
they are preparing to reoccupy their defense positions in depth.
Men are already at work on slit trenches, and others
are digging communication trenches between squads. Work is being done
by groups of three or four men, while another is
posted as guard behind a light machine gun. A detail
is preparing a four-strand barbed wire fence, and others are
bringing up some short logs from the interior, and are
placing them on top of dugouts for buttresses against grenades.
Fire lanes, about two feet above the ground are being
cut in all directions, with concentrations at points where the
trails intersect and where routes of withdrawal have been indicated" . . .
"Are there any weak spots?" . . . "None that I can determine.
It is an all-around defense with no flanks, except the
stream, which may be relatively unprotected, although it's fairly certain
that sniper teams have got the approaches pretty well covered.
Here comes a group of men carrying empty oil drums
and it looks like they will use them for individual
rifle pits by sinking them in the ground flush with
the surface. They plan to place these in a loose,

flexible arc, but heavy machine guns situated at their rear
will give them strong supporting fire. Some Japs are trying
to hide the muzzles with strips of rice straw matting."

You break off. An enemy soldier with an intrenching tool
in his hand is approaching your place of concealment. Watch
him. He hasn't seen you. If he does, get set
to jump up and make a run for it. His
rifle is slung. By the time he's ready to shoot,
Egan and you can be twenty feet away, streaking for
cover. After that, you'll have to rely on the general
confusion to prevent your capture. Here he is. What's he
looking around for? This is the time to crawl into
your helmet until only your feet stick out. What if
he feels like taking a piss? No, he's looking for
loose soil. He stoops over and jabs his spade into
a pile of debris. You can reach out and goose
him if you want to. He's that close. Now he
grabs a handful of grass from a point an arm's
length from your nose, and rips it up by the
roots and you can hear each separate blade being torn
from the earth. He straightens erect again and turns around
and walks away to his hole with the dirt-laden shovel
and the tufts of long grass. You expel your breath.

Fear passes. But it leaves a record of its stay.

41

"Captain MacDonald, this place is getting too hot for us. We're going to pull out." . . . "Do you think you can traverse the fortified area and find out what's doing beyond it, or do you feel you'd have to come back?" . . . "I already know what's behind me, sir." . . . "All right, but don't take any fool chances. Remember your mission. Avoid all contact, and keep your ears and eyes open." . . . "Yes, sir." . . .

You draw your feet up under you and assume a
half-crawling, half-crouching walk, making yourself as small as possible.
       Egan
wants to know what you are going to do, and
you indicate the ravine and tell him that the plan
is to follow the defile right through the defense positions
and report on further enemy preparations. The tall grass, vines
and foliage close in on you from both sides of
the natural crevice like the structural steel framework of buildings
toppling down. "We're moving, Captain. The slope of the hill
is becoming quite pronounced, and the top of this gully
is rather uneven." . . . "Can we use it as a route
of approach?". . ."No. You'd have to travel single file, and
as soon as the Japs get their snipers posted, anyone
taking a Sunday stroll here will be vitamins for worms.". . .
Egan is to your left and he moves along the
ground with a peculiar, mechanical motion as though someone were
prodding him from behind with a pitchfork. Toy soldiers, you
think. Toy soldiers, both of us. They wound us up
and they sent us out and we can do nothing
to prevent the lifting up and the setting down of
our feet until the mainspring plays itself out and we
topple over, stiff and metallic. No, it doesn't require experience
to be courageous, but it certainly demands plenty of practice,
and there is something innately presumptuous in a democracy that
so confidently believes there are extraordinary qualities in ordinary men.

There is a clump of trees on some rising ground
and you see movement among them. "Sir, there is quite
a bit of activity in a wooded sector just beyond
the Jap defense positions, and I think a sizeable force
is being held in reserve to either cover a general
retreat or counter-attack at the right moment." . . . "Well, it seems
clear from our information back here that they will be
used for an assault of some kind, so we'll take
necessary action. Meanwhile, bypass them and keep on going." . . . "Okay."

The ravine curves widely away at right angles to the
enemy assembly point, and you lose sight of the troops.
They looked like a scrawny bunch, but don't underestimate them.
They are at their best in a surprise maneuver like
the one they seem to be planning, because it gives
them an opportunity for swift, offensive action and tends to
minimize any deficiencies they may have in strength or firepower.
Sometimes they'll send wave after wave at a single point,
and sightseers, souvenir hunters and general kibitzers not actively engaged
can actually stand on the sidelines with no danger whatever.
If the maneuver fails, they will still keep pressing forward
regardless of losses rather than retreat. In the heat of
combat they are given to thoughtless acts of desperation and
a tendency toward hysteria, and they seem quite incapable of
making adjustments to fit a changing set of combat conditions.
Once they commit themselves to a battle plan, they will
repeat it over and over again without trying to devise
anything new or attempting to remedy their increasingly difficult situation.

Then, for want of a better idea, they kill themselves.

42

"We have now passed beyond the point where the Jap troops are assembled, but this little ravine is narrowing down to extinction. We're going to abandon it and cut across to where the hill seems to level out a bit. I can't see any more signs of enemy activity from here, but I doubt if the main force of the detachment has shown itself yet." . . . "About how much farther can you go?" . . . You look at the reel and you estimate the length of its coils. "About 75 yards." . . . "Okay, then. But don't use up too much of the wire zigzagging around. Keep to a fairly straight course and don't take unnecessary chances. Remember, we've got other patrols working in the same general area, and if one of them is discovered it will make it tough for everybody. How does the ground look? Do you see any more defense positions?" . . . "No. There are considerably less trees in this part of the slope, and the Japs are using it as an approach route to their fortified line down below. When we stand perfectly still we can hear them passing along the trail. For some reason, they are not especially cautious. I doubt if they even have scouts on the flanks or in front." . . . "Pretty snifty, eh? Where are they coming from?" . . . "I don't think the noise is from above. They seem to be headed this way from some place along the side of the hill." . . . "Is there a bivouac area around there?" . . . "I couldn't say, but the terrain is suitable." . . . "I see. There's a big blank space in my chart between the positions facing Beach Blue and their apparent line of departure here. I wish to hell I could find out what's going on in between." . . . "We'll do all we can, Captain." . . . You cannot quite comprehend the enemy's immediate strategy. It's like looking at a crossword puzzle and finding that it makes sense when you read it horizontally, but also adds up to proper meaning when you read it down. There are no printed programs and all events are unscheduled, and whatever

happens is the end product of the stupendous manufacturing process
wherein millions of actions are performed by millions of men.

Many wars have been fought and a few armistices have
been concluded, and that peace which we have crucified will
never come again for our redemption. Nevertheless, we do not
hold that life is so short that we must do
everything possible to make it shorter, and even in defeat
we can go back. But not the enemy. There is
no place in his homeland for the dishonored Jap soldier,
and when a man is unaccounted for, though he be
missing or captured, his family receives notice of his death.

You'd call it enthusiasm if you agreed with it, fanaticism
because you don't. But it's the thing that makes him
into the tough little guy he is. Always beware of
little guys. Like Napoleon. Like Hitler. Like Hirohito. They're sore
about their stature and it makes them ugly and vengeful.
It makes them cunning and resourceful, too, and their methods
of fighting are like jiu-jitsu, with surprise and mobility substituted
for massed strength. They avoid the slugging match and they
try to strike when the blow is unexpected, and they
do battle with a mixture of military art and vainglorious
audacity and their units are not withdrawn until they are
completely annihilated. Pugnacity, to a Jap, is its own reward,
but each of his coins has a hole in it.

If fanaticism didn't exist it would have to be invented.

43

Egan halts and is instantly alert. From off to your
right there has come the sound of singing. Singing! First
with a few voices and then with the deeper, throatier
swelling of many more. It is incongruous and unaccountable and
singularly out of place. Egan looks at you and mutters,
"What do the Japs think this is—Gilbert and Sullivan?"

"Captain, the Nips are singing some kind of a song." . . .
"Singing? Hold the mouthpiece so I can hear it." . . . You
do as he directs, creeping toward the sound. Through the
trees you can make out the blurred outline of human
forms gathered together in small groups. Captain MacDonald is saying,
"That's the Banzai they're singing. They always do it before
attacking. Just like savages hopping themselves up." . . . "But if they're
going to attack, why are they occupying their defensive positions?" . . .
"That's what I want you to find out. Can you
get any closer?" . . . "I'm about ten yards away now. If
they keep up that racket I'll be able to crawl
right into their second tenor section without being noticed." . . . "Good.
Tell me everything that goes on." . . . You insinuate your way
past clumps of fern and over the large, leathery leaves
of ground-hugging plants. Egan is over to your left, making
for a patch of heavy growth. You try to move
with your body supported on your elbows and knees. Here's
a good spot, well screened without seriously limiting your visibility.

"This is about as near to them as I dare
to go." You speak softly, cloaking your voice with a
hand. The chant is rising in loudness and intensity and
the men are swaying with the fervor of their incantation.
This is screwy. This is haywire. This is something out
of a pulp magazine with a girl in red tights
on the cover being readied for strange, ritualistic torture by
the high priests of a secret cult. But there it
is. Real, live Japs, wasting the most valuable moments of
their lives invoking their honorable ancestors for strength in battle.

Egan kicks your outstretched leg. You twist your head. He
is extremely agitated, and points to his helmet and then
toward the enemy soldiers. From your position you cannot see
any point higher than the waistline of the Jap closest
to you, but by craning your neck and extending your
shoulders slightly you are able to observe a foot or
two above. "Holy mother of God! They're wearing American helmets!"
You can barely control your voice. "The bastards are wearing
our tin hats!" Captain MacDonald is icily calm. "So that's
it. Infiltration. The sons of bitches will try to get
among us and do their dirty work before they're discovered.
It's an old trick. But you can bet every one
of them will be carrying a coffin on his back."

The singing has stopped. There is an expectant hush and
all eyes are centered on an officer who has appeared
from one side. He is a little taller than the
others and his manner is imposing and deliberate. "Looks like
the commander is getting set to take over." . . . "What is
he doing?" . . . "Well, right now he's glaring pretty viciously in
the direction of the beach. He just yelled something that
sounded like 'Chikusho' and all the boys are repeating it" . . .
"That's a curse word. It means damned animal." . . . "Now he's
got his fist up in the air and he's screaming
something else. 'Yaruzo.' " . . . "That means Let's do it." . . . "Everybody
    stamping
with their feet and lifting up their rifles and shouting."

They are a means in search of a justified end.

44

"The floorshow seems to be over now. They're breaking up their little act and going their separate ways, although they seem to know what they're doing. Here come some of them down the trail carrying an unwieldy looking object. It might be a field piece of sorts, but it seems rather elongated. Hell no, it's not a gun, it's a . . ." You pause while your mind attempts to grasp what your eyes are telling it. "It's a boat! It's an assault craft! Just like the ones we use for river crossings and stuff." . . . "Great God! Why in heaven's name . . ." The captain's voice drops off, then comes back strong and rapid. "I've got it! I see it all now. They're going down to the water, probably at a point between beaches Red and Blue, and will launch an amphibious attack. They'll sneak up behind us and land exactly where we did and try to cut us off from the rear. They'll do everything possible to look like a bunch of Americans from the shore, so they won't arouse any suspicion. Naturally, they won't be fired on because our men are coming in all the time. Oh, my aching ass! How could we have been so dumb? That's why they made things so easy for us. Listen. Can you see how many boats they have?" . . . "I don't know. I counted four already, but they're jammed up one behind the other all along the trail. Some of the men are carrying small outboard motors and others are lugging rubber containers made buoyant with balsa floats, which will probably be used to send supplies in to shore. There are about twenty men assigned to every boat, and at least one of them has a flame thrower. As far as I can determine, each unit is under the command of an officer, and more of an effort is being made toward jungle discipline. They've quieted down quite a bit and apparently expect to achieve complete surprise." . . .

You hear a strangled distortion over the telephone and then silence. "Did you say something, Captain?" There is no answer

and your mind is bludgeoned with comprehension. They cut it!
They must have found the wire and snipped it. Get
out of here! Leave the reel and the handset behind.
They'll pounce on the area in a minute, if they
haven't got you surrounded already. Egan is watching you apprehensively.
"They found the wire. Help me get this damned harness
off, will you?" He squirms to your side and together
you unfasten the buckles. Your hands are trembling. Hurry. Hurry.
Over your head now. You shove the telephone equipment into
the bushes. You hear the sound of approaching feet, and
your heart runs down to the cellar of your being
three steps at a time. Frantically you churn through the
leaves and the stems and the thorns and the twining
roots. Which way? Any way, as long as it separates
you from the Japs on the trail and your pursuers
behind you. There's an open stretch ahead. Run across it
and maybe they won't notice you because everybody looks like
an American around here anyhow. But they'll spot Egan. He's
tall. Oh, Christ, what a time to be tall. Your
legs are free and they catapult you into the clearing.
There is a yell and you hear a shot and
the high-pitched whirr of a bullet. A vine cracks you
across the face, but your sensations are dulled and edgeless
and any feelings you may have are strictly from memory.

So much of your past still lies ahead of you.

45

Your whole body is battered by little shocks of instinct
and your mind is loose and unbuttoned and all your
thinking is drained from you in disjointed blobs. There's some
uneven ground a bit to your right, and you make
for it, but you see that there is a barrier
of trees on either side of it and that the
space between is narrowed down like a funnel, but you
can't stop yourself. A Jap with a pistol runs out
into the trail and he shoots at you and darts
quickly back and then the whole place kicks and scratches
at you with bullets and then suddenly the earth jumps
up and slams into your chest and crashes you down.

Egan is lying at your side and his mouth is
working as if he were trying to swear, but it
is clogged by a jumble of obscenities and all he
can say is, "Why—you—Goddam—." You are afraid that
he might lose his head and start shooting and you
fling your arm across his elbows so that he cannot
move them to lift his Garand. "Shut up! Shut up!"

There is a reserve of coolness holding your muscles together.
You know that you have been surrounded and that the
enemy has cut off your escape route to the rear.
But the wildness of their fire tells you that they
cannot see you where you are lying and that they
are only guessing at your likely position of concealment in
the hope that you will reveal yourself by crying out
or by returning their shots. You can see a few
of them peering out from behind tree trunks and bushes
with their sallow, hairy faces marked with the stalker's boldness.

The Japs are forming into a human noose and will
close in on you from all sides. They deliberately stumble
over matted vines and remnants of logs and expose themselves

for fleeting moments. They are a chain of men moving
in a series of sidesteps while steadily eyeing suspected areas.

Egan mutters, "Are we going to lay here and let
them stand over us and shoot us like a couple
of trapped rats? Jesus Christ!" You say, "I don't think
He's interested. Why should He be? He was expendable, too."
You are listening to yourself talk as though the words
were coming from some other lips. Egan is caustic. "Goddamit,
this isn't a movie at post theatre number one. This
is us. Maybe in books a guy can sit around
gargling his philosophical mouthwash when he's sweating out a transfer
to the pearly gates, but not for me." Your voice
is slightly raised. "You sound like a man with a
paper asshole. Don't you think I'd like to shoot my
way out of this if I thought it could be
done?" He turns his head anxiously. "They're forty yards away
from us. Forty lousy yards." You look around. "If there's
a blind spot somewhere, we could make a break for
it. The best thing to do is head for their
own lines because they won't expect us to move in
that direction. You go first, and I'll cover you with
the Tommy gun. Go ahead!" He rises on his knees
and springs up and away. There is a shot. Egan
jerks erect and emits a rasping scream and blood spurts
from his neck. Three more rifles crack and he falls
backward a few yards from you with his helmet bashed
in and his substance trickling out of the metal fissures.

There's a corner of your mind that'll never sleep again.

46

You swing your body around so that you face the
source of the Japanese fire, and you lift up the
Tommy gun and level it at a clump of bushes
that are still oscillating from enemy muzzle blasts. You are
angry. You are more angry now than you have ever
been in your life, and in your furious energy you
press the trigger until you feel that it has pierced
the skin of your forefinger. You are firing in a
single, continuous burst and you spray the treetrunks and the
rocks and the rises in the ground with a wild
whiplash of lead. The gun is getting hot and your
flesh becomes prickly and your shoulder is throbbing with the
recoil, but you keep on shooting until the ammunition drum
gives out and there is only the dull click of
the breeching mechanism. The noise is cleft and there is
gaping silence. That's all, brother. That's all. No more ammo.
You've had your fling and now they can come and
ring your doorbell and tell you that the men are
here to remove the corpses. You look toward Egan and
you see him twisted into an agonized posture, inflexible and
stony, like a personal monument to pain. He is in
blood an inch deep and it has darkened the earth
in an irregular blotch. You roll over into a small
depression next to him. See if he's alive. See if
anything can be done for him. Even if it's only
a gesture. Even if it's the last thing you do.

You stretch out your hand and place it over his
heart and you flatten your palm against his shirt, hoping
to catch a beat, a flutter, a vibration, a throb.
But there is only the sodden dampness of his sweat
and the thin tingle of human warmth turning to coldness.

He is dead in his own blood and in his
own shadow. This is light to pallor and flame to
cinder and fruit to dry core. You liked this man.

You liked the way his mouth opened when he smiled
and the asterisks that were formed in the corners of
his eyes and his large nose like a strong handle
for his face. And now the quietness of other eternities.

Maybe you should have told him that you had been
hit. Maybe you should have pointed to the wound in
your hip that now feels wet and clammy and stings
like a hot pincers and said that your whole side
was numb and paralyzed and that was why you couldn't
make a break for it. Then he would have stayed
behind and not tried to escape the ambush. But if
there was any chance of getting away, you wanted him
to have it and so you controlled your breathing and
kept your voice normal and hoped he wouldn't notice that
agony was walking across your face without wiping its shoes.

The Japs must have seen you moving, but they are
wary about exposing themselves because of your submachine gun. That's
a good one. That's rich. Afraid of an empty Tommy.
But you've still got a grenade in your shirt pocket
and enough hatred left in your arm to throw it,
so let them come. Your eyes focus momentarily on a
rifle barrel drawing a bead on you from some shrubs
and you duck your head. There is a shot and
Egan's body quivers and you gulp your breath down quickly.
Then another Jap fires and another and another and another.

You want to be brave. You also want to be.

47

The Japs are encouraged by your failure to return their
fire, and they probably suspect that you have been hurt.
You see one of them warily emerge from behind a
tree and move noiselessly toward you. The grenade is in
your right hand and the finger of your left hooks
the safety pin and withdraws it. Another enemy soldier is
advancing on you from a point off to one side.
Throw it! Throw it! You thrust the grenade along the
ground with a sweeping sidearm motion and you watch it
bounce like a booted football and carom off a root
and roll into some fallen leaves with a dry rustle.
The nearest Jap has seen it, and he springs forward
as though to pick it up, but he cannot find
it and he turns back and frantically waves his arms
and runs. The explosion blows up the earth all around
you and you keep your head low to escape the
fragmentation. You hear a yelp and the thud of a
body falling and the sound of confused feet. Then quiet.

Your face is jammed into your elbow, and you slowly
raise your eyes to see over it, when a second
and more powerful blast knocks your forehead into the dirt.
It seemed to have come from behind you and your
dazed mind asks, wonderingly, "Did I do that?" only you
know that the enemy is probably tossing all they have
in your direction. But what's all the shouting for? What's
all the commotion and the rushing around and the hubbub
and the tumult? There is another eruption, this time a
little closer, and you are sure you heard the whine
of a shell above all the voices. Artillery fire! From
the beach! From us! Now they'll get it! Now these
bastards and whorelovers will get what they've been asking for!

The boys must have debarked the guns and set them
up on shore and begun laying down a barrage in
preparation for a continued push inland. Again a shell screeches

overhead and the air crackles with its passage and the
hillside reverberates with upheaval. A whistle sounds somewhere down below
and the jarring quaver of voices stops and there is
only the strident tones of someone giving frenzied orders. Are
they assembling? Feet are pounding the turf as though men
were approaching rapidly. Two of them. Maybe three. And they're
heading your way. You edge close to Egan. Play dead.
Sink your face into the mud and let your arm
dangle limply. Control your muscles. Take a deep breath and
hold it. Here they are. One of them slows down.
He says something excitedly and the others stop. Maybe they'll
stab you. Maybe they'll shoot you. You feel him standing
over Egan. He kicks him in the shoulder, and the
force of the blow sends his helmet dully clanging against
your own. Another shell whirrs downward and quakes the earth,
and again you hear the whistle through your fogged ears.
One of the other Japs speaks, and his manner is
urgent. He starts trotting away and is followed by the
third. The first soldier hesitates momentarily and then moves off,
anxiously calling on his comrades to wait up for him.

You let your air out and open your eyes. Well,
you have been spared, and by every reasoning you should
feel relieved and exalted. But all you can experience is
a profound indifference and a deepening lassitude and a sense
of boredom and weariness and even a little of resentment.

Life's a luxury. You can't afford luxuries on Army pay.

48

The Japs are getting ready to evacuate the area, and
you are alone with Egan. The boom of the field
pieces and howitzers from the shore is becoming more frequent
as additional guns are beached and brought into position to
shell the places where reconnaissance patrols have reported enemy concentrations

The wound in your side is throbbing and the cloth
of your jungle suit feels like sandpaper against it. You
are having difficulty drawing breath, and your lungs make a
snoring, sibilant sound as they fill with air. Your mind
is flogged with self-preservation and keeps repeating, "Get out of
here, get out of here, do you want to be
hit by your own guns?" But your body accepts only
one problem at a time, and it says, "Don't crowd,
don't push, don't rush me. I am slowly coming to
a stop like a wheel revolving on a roller bearing
and I refuse to let anything interrupt my leisurely momentum."

You wonder if there is such a thing as a
physical desire for death, and whether it is just as
strong as the will to live. Isn't there an urge,
a force, a basic compulsion to lead organic matter back
into the inorganic state, and by so doing re-establish a
pattern that was abnormally disturbed by the emergence of life?
After all, what is your body to you? You fed
it, you clothed it, you washed it, you cared for
it and you told it that it was you. But
when its walled passageway narrows down and miles become yards
and yards feet and feet inches, you find to your
amazement how little you set by it. It's trivial. Unimportant.
Birth seems to have been goodbye to some inanimate entity
and only the logical end of living is hello again.

And yet, why not save yourself if you can? Why
not? Drag yourself out of immediate danger and make your

way back to friendly territory! Only Egan can talk about
death with any certainty. You have known nothing but living.

You look at him for the last time before shifting
in the direction of safety. You start your thoughts working
and turn away and leave them thinking. "I'll be seeing
you, Ege. I'll be seeing you. There must be some
place where there are no restrictions, space unreckoned, time unclocked,
where two beings advancing in a parallel can defy the
laws of earthly mathematics and actually meet. And so, until
my shadow, rounding a corner on a street in Paradise,
bumps into yours and with a beg your pardon starts
to hurry away, but suddenly wheels and shouts and joins
you in glad recognition . . . Okay, kid. I'll be seeing you.

"And in the meantime, God, treat him well because he's
very tired and I happen to know he didn't sleep
last night. Give him everything he wants that he couldn't
get down here because the PX closed too early. But
don't make him stand around or sit or kneel or
stoop. Let him march. Always let him march. I was
at the rear in our squad formations and he was
in front of me, and I know he loved to
march because of the way he held his head and
swung his arms. So let him march, God. The sun
marches and the clouds march and the stars march and
the world marches. Make him a part of all that
marching. Out into the sky let him march, rhythmically, unendingly,
proudly, victoriously. Hut, tupe, trip, pfaw. . . . Hut, tupe, trip, pfaw.

"And wherever he is, that's the head of the column."

49

You are beginning to hear the sound of rifle shots,
sometimes wide apart and sometimes in a continuous crackle, like
a flame taking hold of a dry log. Occasionally the
shooting is joined by protracted machine gun bursts, or is
strikingly underlined by exploding hand grenades and eruptive mortar shells,
and beyond them you hear the artillery from the beach
as the guns continue to drop their loads of H.E.

There is an odd, frightening beauty in motion against fixity.
Howitzer projectiles arch gracefully like a chorus girl's gilded heel,
then blow up the simile, strewing syllables in little bits.
And the rush of bursting traffic overhead produces strange embroidery
until concussion somersaults your blood so that it flows backwards
and you see your bulging heart with eyes turned in.

The boys must be moving out. They must have gotten
orders to resume the advance. Through the lens of imagination
you see them going forward, crouching, running, dodging, creeping, falling.
There's your company, your platoon, your squad. There's Captain MacDonald
and Lt. Nixon, Lloyd, Graham, Chapman, Ivey, Whitney. And there's—
no, not Lindstrom. And not Egan either, or Shearer, or
Simmons or the Mouse. But wait a minute. Who says
they're not there? And who says you're not there, either?
Sure, you're there. Everybody's there. Everybody contributes something. The
          thought
of the dead and wounded makes it easier for fighting
men to kill. It's a push. It's a shove. They've
seen their buddies die horribly, and that's the most pitiable
sight in all human experience. And so they translate their
grief into anger, scorn, fury. When the dust of horizontal
heroes can mingle with charging feet, the dead lie still.

This is the showdown, all right. This is the payoff.
We'll win. Sure, we'll win. Everybody is certain of victory
and no one thinks of losing. Everybody fights with a
cold wrath and nobody fears death. The closer it comes

to them the less they fear it. And that is
because they are alive and the very function of being
alive is to repeat over and over again, "Death is
not for me, death is not for me. Others may
die, but I will go on indestructibly. I will live."

But do they ever stop to realize in how many
places a man can be hit? Head, neck, shoulders, arms,
hands, chest, ribs, stomach, abdomen, groin, back, buttocks, thighs, knees,
legs, feet. And did they ever see a wounded man
suffer? No, it isn't the heart that dies last, it
is the eyes. Two small eyes, each about a quarter
of an inch in diameter, covering in all a total
area of no more than just a fraction. And yet
they can hold every single bit of misery the world
has ever had without spilling so much as a tear.

Well, then—call it an occupational hazard. There are causes
of death, just as there are causes of life. Battle
is a cause of death and should be considered along
with cancer, tuberculosis and pneumonia and any other fatal disease.
And who here can place any value whatever on life
when the mere incidence of oblivion can reduce it from
the pinnacle of pricelessness to a few coppers' worth of
minerals and dross, salt and fertilizer? That's the rate of
exchange in universal currency, and if you speak of imponderables
or potentials or any other set of values, nobody will
know what you are talking about because all they can
recognize is the basic and the tangible reality of non-existence.

With a bit of practice almost anyone can be extinct.

There is a lull in the artillery barrage while the
guns seem to shift gears. And in the comparative quiet,
the small arms fire to the front of you is
even louder and more intense. Attack. Defense. Counterattack. Retreat. Pursuit.
Just words, words, words. Put them all together and what
do they add up to? A soldier. An anonymous guy
in a uniform. A body without a face. A number
without a name. A statistic coming to grips with the
enemy. A card in an index file bleeding to death.

G.I. Joe, they call him. "G.I. Joe," they say, as
if it were something cute and cunning to be smiled
at patronizingly. Sure, lots of laffs. Plenty of jokes. The
grinning kid. That's Joe. Ain't he a fetching little fella?

If all there was to it was just washing his
socks in his helmet. If all there was to it
was just spending a night in a foxhole. If all
there was to it was just eating the same tasteless
rations out of a can three times a day. If
all there was to it was just swinging down a
road while the Public Relations Office photographer took his picture—
then he would believe the people who say how magnificent
he is and how full of good humor he remains
and how he is conducting himself through a dirty business
with the dignity and courage and laughter of an American.

But it's more than just that. It's a sharp cry
held in a muted throat. It's seeing your buddy shot
and listening to him breathe and watching his final movements.
It's never having quite enough of everything at one time.
If you've got a cigaret, nobody's got a match. If
you've got a match, nobody's got a cigaret. If you
have a razor, you find that your blades are unusable.
If you have good blades, someone has borrowed your razor.
If you have both razor and blades you discover that

you have lost your shaving cream. And if you have
all three you're told there's no water for shaving anyway.

It's a compound fracture of the illusions, an intimate hell
where a corpse dances on a firelit wall, a lonely
night that sobs itself to sleep, a demented hunchback babbling
to himself in the dark, a tuneless piano with half
of its keys missing, a blind man lost between stars
on his way to God, a wild, shrieking ride on
a runaway nightmare, a spirit perpetually sagging at half mast.

Someday they'll put up a big monument to it in
memory of those boys who fell during the course of
its being, and it will be made of marble with
bronze statuary and a high-sounding inscription cut into the sides.
But if Joe had his way, he'd tear it down
and melt the statues and let the marble crumble under
indignant sledges. Oh, yes—he'd put up a war monument
all right. It would be a little plot of ground
in the middle of the main drag, fenced in by
barbed wire, and in the center of it there would
be a drainage ditch dug with a pole over it
and a crudely lettered sign saying "Latrine." And all the
Joes would come and urinate in it and empty their
bowels in it and throw garbage in it and fill
it with red liquid that looks like blood. And people
would watch it flowing like a public fountain and they
would smell it and they would be reminded of war.

But you can't submerge tragedy that takes lessons in swimming.

51

Joe's coming. With every moment passed and every shot fired,
Joe is coming. He's just a steadily advancing line on
a map showing where the fighting is. And he's coming.

Follow the roadsigns, Joe. Keep to the right. Observe the
local speed limits. Go slow on dangerous curves. Don't turn
into any blind alleys. Watch the guy in front of
you. Don't jam up. It's one way traffic, Joe. It's
forward only. But the lights, Joe, watch the lights. Some
of them are green, and that's okay. But the others
are bloodcolored and that means stop, and when it happens
you'll wait a long time for the lights to change.

There are traffic cops too, Joe, and they keep you
moving and see to it that you don't run out
of gas and give you directions whether you need them
or not and write out a ticket if you do
something they think is wrong. They're on your side, Joe,
but they represent a system of regularity and conformity that
has become bigger than they are and bigger than you
are and bigger than anything you ever thought was human.

And so they sit in rooms that are far away
and point to charts on the wall and indicate little
bits of tinted paper stuck in a sandbox, and say,
"Take this island, envelop that position, break through right here."
And nobody's legs give way under them, and nobody starts
coughing and spitting blood, and nobody carries in a boy
that's too old to cry and too young to swear
and too lifeless for either. And nobody sticks him in
the sand and says, "This is Joe," while all the
traffic cops present nod their heads in agreement and murmur,
"Yes, General, yes indeed, General, how right you are, General."

So that's the end of Joe. And all the people
at home hear that Joe is gone and they are

sorry it happened and they add, "Gee, he never told
me that he was in any kind of danger, you
should see his letters, they sound so full of jokes
and anecdotes and stuff you'd think he was vacationing at
some country club with a bunch of his college chums."
But what do they expect? Do they think that Joe
is going to tell them what he's been through and
what he expects to go through and all the things
that he doesn't even dare to tell himself? It's a
feeling he has that can't be expressed in V-mail letters,
the way one thought builds on another until it extends
all the way to the front door, only it sounds
weak and silly and sentimental when it's said out loud,
and what in hell is there to write about anyway?

It's all routine. The slogging along in mud, the feel
of the rifle on your shoulder, the crudeness of sanitation,
the griping, the personal discomforts. Those things aren't ever important.
So he spent a week in a foxhole. So what?
So he covered seventy miles in two days. So what?
So he killed a whole company of Japs and rescued
every one of his buddies from certain extinction. So what?
Here's what really matters to him: a paved street lined
with familiar trees and a grassy lawn and a car
and a girl and a hamburger joint and a crowd
coming out of a movie and a hot bath and
a gay necktie and the labor of a trolley going
uphill and a glossy pond and peanuts behind third base.

It isn't the war that bothers him. It's the duration.

52

It's funny how a bunch of Joes can endure all
this and still keep a tight hold on the continuity
of normal living. They know that what they left was
not ideal and what they will go back to will
not be ideal and that the chances are they will
never live to see anything ideal ever realized. But they
know that what they had was substantially better than what
they have now, and they trust their memories to relinquish
the bad and retain and even improve upon the good.

And so they talk and think and dream of a
scheme of things they would like to fit themselves into,
and even though a tabulation of their desires would seem
like a compendium of trivia, it all adds up to
what is necessary and fitting and worth their holding onto.
The words they use to express these sentiments are in
the accents of the North and the South and the
Middlewest and the Southwest and New England and the coast,
and they are the blasphemous and obscene and the terrifyingly
simple words that men use when they can't quite put
their fingers on what they mean and when they haven't
got time for fancy stuff and when the immediate events
are in themselves too heavy with drama for elaborate dramatics.

Nobody stands up and strikes an attitude and says, "This
is what I'm fighting for." All the phrases, all the
mouthings, all the ideas in the world are patently ridiculous
when the only thing that counts is keeping alive from
one day to the next. And why should it be
a matter of conjecture in the first place about why
they are fighting? They are grown men, not driveling morons
or romantic poets or analytical highbrows. They don't need a
glib spokesman to tell them that their country is involved
in a war and that in accordance with a legal
provision they have been called upon to fight that war.
It's like paying a license fee or filing an income

tax return or respecting the value of a piece of
paper that claims to be a dollar. It's law, it's
government, it's a duty of citizenship. To them it's absurd
and wholly unreasonable to say that they have traveled five
thousand miles to protect their homes and families when they
know perfectly well they could have better homes and happier
families by not going anywhere at all. Ask a Jap
what he fights for and he will tell you that
he has also come a long way to protect his
home and family. So there you have it. Americans and
Japs fighting for the things they had before they started
to fight and giving them up in order to fight
for them. Christ, it doesn't make sense. The ordinary American
wants no part of a Jap's house, and the common
Jap would be miserable living in America. And yet one
of them commits an act of aggression in response to
an order, and the other rises to retaliate in accordance
with national conscription and they both endeavor to kill each
other when commanded to do so. There are little people
and there are big people, and the little people are
in the overwhelming majority, but just the same they always
do what the big people tell them to do. And
that is at once the silliest and the most outrageously
impertinent form of tyranny the world has ever known, for
it is the persecution of the many by the few.

Battle doesn't determine who is right. Only who is left.

53

All that noise. All that Goddam noise. It's like the
whirr and clatter of a giant industrial plant busy filling
a big war contract. The battle starts at one end
of the assembly line and gets larger and larger as
it goes along. And the men who fight the battle
are the mechanical parts on the machinery that conveys it
forward, and they mesh and interconnect in response to movements
of cams and gears and piston rods. But some of
them expose a wearing surface or become worn down through
friction or are burned out by constant use or develop
cracks from fatigue, and they are taken off and inspected
to see if they can possibly be repaired or salvaged.
And if they can't be put back in place, then
they are discarded and spares are requisitioned from the stockroom.

The battle goes on. It is picked up and set
down and something is added to it and it is
shifted over to one side and a complete new unit
is mounted on it and the bolts are fitted in
place and the screws are tightened. Right now you can't
recognize it because the whole framework has not been assembled
and there are lots of appliances and accessories that are
yet to come. But when it finally rolls off the
belts and conveying equipment and comes to a full stop,
you'll see the very latest model in high powered meatchoppers.

Listen. Listen to the blades threshing and the wheels gnashing,
and the grinding that goes around and around and around.
It's battle. It's war. It's the Army. No, it's not
the Army of the parade ground or the drill field
or the barracks, with clean sheets every seven days and
three percent beer at the service club and weekend passes.
This is the meatchopper army, where everything is reduced to
a fluid pulp and all of living is a mass
of oily stickiness that heaves and boils and drags its
clogged elements down into it. That other army taught men

to walk erect. In this one they learn to crawl.
That other army made men practice movements in group formation.
In this one they are alone and they move singly.
That other army demanded straight lines and the smoothest ground.
In this one, traversing an open area is sure suicide.
That other army insisted on polished brass. In this one
the glint of metal will cost a man his life.

That other army taught men that a pair of shined
shoes at inspection was more important than all humanitarian ideals
put together, that a dustfree footlocker carried more weight with
the company commander than three college degrees and that a
shortorder cook with a bar on his shoulder was more
to be respected than the wisest man in the world.

In this army, men learn how to be friendly and
tolerant and how to master the science of getting along
and working together. Discipline expresses itself in freedom, and leadership
comes from a source within themselves and understanding is the
result of experiences shared. They know what is just and
sincere and they hate sham and fraud and broken promises.
They know their own weaknesses and they know that nothing
lasts and events are unpredictable. And best of all, they
are beginning to realize that they have weight and mass
and power and strength enough to enforce the basic integrity
they need and admire, so that the leaders they trust
are in the long run accountable to those who follow.

They stumble over truth but continue as if nothing happened.

54

You are trying to give yourself a good excuse for
being here. You feel that someone has demanded an explanation
and that you've been called upon to rationalize a meatchopper.
And in your befuddlement you lose the trend of the
arguments you were going to use, and stammer and search
despairingly for one word to follow another in orderly meaning.
You start by asking questions that you cannot answer, and
you end up by answering questions that you haven't asked.

"God in His infinite wisdom. . . . God in His infinite wisdom."
It's a beautiful phrase, and even if you accept it
as being more than beauty, there must be many things
He cannot know. Surely, among all the millions of worlds
that He has scattered into space, there must be one
whose records have been misplaced and who has failed to
stand each morning's formation without being marked **AWOL**. Surely among
so many there must be one that He would overlook
on his regular tours of inspection and for whom His
search would be abandoned in the press of other affairs.
Surely, there must be one whose events are haphazard coincidences
and whose history is a combination of accidents and whose
immediate destiny is largely in the hands of its inhabitants.

Some of these inhabitants have a special code by which
they live, and others have only the simple, realistic credo
of unorganized vegetation. Some of them build meatchoppers, methodically,
       fanatically,
and they think that the solution to all their ills
lies in the construction of a bigger one than was
ever built before. Others try to disassemble the mechanism and
destroy it and seek out the blueprints and put them
to the torch, but the battlecries they utter are words
they only vaguely know and the hopes they attempt to
redeem have never been fulfilled and the principles they extol
have but rarely been practiced. They have what they call
democracy and they are content to let it muddle along

like a spoiled child, wasting its time and money and
making mistake after mistake with amiable caprice but preserving its
health by declining to worry. And the only reason it
survives is that it is inherently optimistic and no matter
how bleak the outlook, it would never contemplate its self-destruction.

But what do they intend doing when the meatchopper has
been torn down? Will they go right on habitually tinkering
with the same old defective parts and excavate in the
same old insecure foundation and just give it a new
coat of paint and name it something else? There are
lots of inhabitants who have been valiantly butting their brows
against its structure until they have become unconscious and fallen
into a deep dream in which everything was cleared away
and a bright edifice miraculously arose. And when they awaken
they want to feel that they have become a part
of that dream and that a pleasantly furnished room awaits
them with a soft, luxurious bed and an adjacent bath.

They don't know how it will come about, but they
know that it will happen. It won't be a shining
sword coming down out of the sky, and it won't
be a paid advertisement in a newspaper and it won't
be a burning bush and it won't be a single
man or a single idea or even a new kind
of veterans' organization. But they are sure of its coming
and they are certain that when it arrives it will
be more like having a reunion than greeting a stranger.

Happiness is a good thing. Somebody ought to start it.

55

There is the dull rumble of tanks and the shooting
is settling down to a devil's tattoo. From the shore
there is a great roar developing, and you wonder if
maybe the Jap amphibious counter-offensive has been intercepted by the
Navy's guns. Planes are aloft again, veering full throttle and
swooping low to strafe the enemy craft approaching the beach.

Blood from the wound in your side still seeps through
your clothing and dampens the earth, but the pain has
numbed itself and you are able to observe your body
with vague disinterest, like a poor substitute for a mother.
Darkness seems to be crawling all around you and little
gusts of heat tumble over the ground and the trees
are jibbering with flecked mouths of green and space is
split with trembling. There is a climactic staccato of rifles
from below and the noise of running through underbrush and
the exultant shouts of pursuit. Your brain tries to attract
your attention, tugging at the sleeves of your senses to
say that the enemy has broken from his positions and
is retreating along the base of the hill. But your
spirit merely nods with a weary indifference and tells it
that you are tired of men and their petty problems
and their writhing efforts to survive and the frail flesh
and its tenuous hold on perpetuity. You want to be
alone in this penultimate solitude, this last but one, and
take the stopper out of memory and let it spill.

This is the summing up, the thumbing over, the sorting
out, the placing together in neat piles what is in
the mind and what is in the heart. *To everything
there is a season. A time to be born and
a time to die. A time to embrace and a
time to refrain from embracing. A time for war and
a time for peace.* So be it. So be it.

You were arbitrarily placed between the rigid brackets of birth
and death, and in between you grow and develop and

you go from one end of it to the other
without being able to turn back and retrace your footsteps.
You never felt strange about being alive, about finding yourself
equipped with arms and legs and physical functions, about seeing
things, recognizing colors, feeling heat and cold, touching objects, experiencing
events. Maybe it was a little odd and uncomfortable in
the beginning, but when you stopped being curious it all
righted itself and seemed proper and normal. And yet, there
was something held apart from you, as though you had
outlived the period for which you were born too soon,
and you didn't really belong, and that any minute someone
could be expected to tap you on the shoulder and
ask to see your printed invitation. And so, because you
had crashed the gate and been absorbed in the crowd,
you could never bring yourself to believe in your own
essentialness, and you became a spectator and watched things happen
to others and watched them happen to yourself. And people
thought you were rather dull and lazy, if they noticed
you at all, and said that you didn't give a
damn about what was important and that you would probably
be a failure. And they couldn't seem to understand that
you really weren't trying to be anything in particular, that
you were just a bystander, an eavesdropper, a miscellaneous individual
who didn't talk very much but who was able to
observe a good deal because he always sat in corners.

You matured because you gave all your time to it.

56

You are alone in the hands of recollection and they
caress your skin and beckon to the flesh while the
flesh beckons to the bone. And together they reach out
and build a wall out of sand in order to
imprison thoughts that would never make an effort to escape.

Well, what is there to remember? Of infancy? Of childhood?
An ordinary house with an ordinary tree in an ordinary
back yard. A broken toy and the bright penny in
the tight fist for the square of chocolate and the
bewildering necessity of putting the left shoe on the left
foot. Voices. Pleasant voices, scolding voices, entreating voices, impatient voices.
Voices feeding you, voices fondling you, voices raised to spank.
A walk along a dusty road with hands thrust deep
in pockets and a shrill, tuneless whistle through airconditioned teeth.
Schooling and the terrible shyness and the awareness of self.
A game, a book, a friendship, a hill and the
clamorous joy of running down it, and the knowledge of
a secret spot of cool shade. The darkness of night
and the silence and a special star to wish upon.
Years telescoping together and crowding themselves up and the abrupt
realization that no one had ever taught you how to
read the face of a clock. The clannishness of small
boys, the clubbiness, the teaminess, the togetherness of puppy spirits.

Well, has it been any different with your coming of
age? An ordinary foxhole near an ordinary palm in an
ordinary jungle. A useless Tommy gun, a bar of dried
chocolate from a K-ration, and the utter compulsion to lie
on your right side because very little remains of your
left. Voices here, too. Japanese voices yelling in terror. American
voices cursing, growling, some voices striding onward in stalwart tones,
other voices limping quaveringly along with stones in their shoes.
Muddy trails to walk upon, to crawl upon and to
sink down under, and hands that are raised in a
signal meaning stop or swept forward in a sign that

means go or stretched in postures more meaningful than all.
And there are whistles, also without tune, that signify retreat
to some and charge to others and let loose a
million acts of unthinking bravery. A Yank hears them and
he says, "Here goes nothing." A Jap hears them too,
and he cries, "Kimi ga yo!" (rule a thousand years)
and begs the Emperor to excuse the length of his
life as he hadn't time to live a short one.

There is schooling here, and you learn by doing, and
it is the best education there is because you can't
cut any classes. There is poignant introversion in which you
create new accessories to wear with the fears that are
currently in style. There are still the games of hide
and seek, with bullets to truculently declare, "Tag, you're it,"
and a book you surprise yourself quoting from, and the
thought of a friend's face autographed by pain stabs you
in your military secret. There is a hill that you
cannot run down, but must be carried, and cool shade
that subtracts its differential from the body's warmth, and darkness
that comes to blood when the sun dries it, and
a silence you do not break but fit right into.
Clocks are present, snapping their fingers at eternity, and men
who wonder if they were ever boys still think and
act and die together, and the star that you hung
your wishes on is still there somewhere in the sky.

Flat on your back, there's nowhere to look but up.

57

The looping ribbon of memory is coiling itself around you,
drawing closer and closer and ever more pressing until it
feels like a woman's warm hand resting on your cheek.

What is thy beloved more than another beloved? My beloved
is unto me as a bundle of myrrh. Honey and
milk are under her tongue. Her lips are like a
thread of scarlet and her mouth is comely. The joints
of her thighs are like jewels. Her belly is like
a heap of wheat set about with lilies. And I
will make mention of my love more than of wine.

Let your heart make a recording of all the lovelinesses
that she has given you, and let it play them
back to you slowly, and let the needle stick occasionally
so that you may hear her say hello again and
again and again and touch your name to her lips.

Always she is waiting for your mind. Always your thoughts
run up the same path and burst through the same
door. Always at the end of thinking her soft fingers
smooth away distraction and the white image of her face
is a cushion for your weariness. How much of hell
you have put away to turn to her. How much
of desolation and sorrow and loneliness she helped you overcome.

Do you remember the last time you saw her on
that final furlough when you didn't have time to tell
her that you would be arriving, and you let yourself
into the house and you sat there waiting like an
empty glass for the bright, bubbly champagne of her coming?
Do you remember the hat she wore and the way
her hair was combed and how the room seemed to
fill up when she entered it, and the look in
her eyes when she saw you and how you had
to tell her to go wipe her face because her

soul was smeared all over it? Do you remember the
thousand little fires you lit each day and how one
by one they were themselves consumed until all you had
left was a special portion of their brilliance for nightly
candles that would always burn in farflung windows? Do you
remember that last parting at the station when you tried
to tell her what you didn't know and you couldn't
level your gaze to hers because it would have meant
talking and you couldn't talk because it would have meant
saying goodbye, and so you held her hand and said
that you were certainly glad it had been nice weather?

Well, here is a nice new day fresh from the
dawn's opaque wrapping paper and the sunlight is getting stronger
and you are beginning to feel its intensity. The locale
has shifted, but it is the same sun rising from
the same direction and depositing the same coin of gold
in the same diurnal slot. She has seen this sun
in the east and she has spoken to it and
it is carrying her message to you and it drops
it down through the trees on its usual journey westward.

So take this bit of luminousness that has fallen from
the sky, and hold it in your hands and lift
it up to your face and drink of it with
your lips until you can't hold any more and it
drips down your chin. This is the glad, enduring flame
you didn't have time to kindle, the warmth that merges
the molten tallow of your separate tapers in bright foreverness.

And you blink because her eyes are in every ray.

58

Let thy garments be always white and let not thy
head lack ointment. Live joyfully with the wife whom thou
lovest all the days of the life of thy vanity.

Get up! Get up! You're going home! Roll out of
that sack and cram your stuff into your barracks bags
and swing 'em on that truck waiting out in front.
You're going where the houses are built the way you
like to see them, and where the streetlamps go on
at night and where a macadam road winds around the
corner and its tar grows hot and sticky in summer
and trees lean over and cool it by breathing softly.
You're going to a place where lights go on when
you push a button and hot meals are served in
china plates and clean water runs at the twist of
your wrist and starched shirts come out of a paper
package and you can sit on a toilet seat in
privacy, and walk erect without fear and say good night
to friends and know that you will see them alive
some other time, and take your wife in your arms
without a schedule of train departures in your hip pocket.

Stop it! Stop it! You're crazy, you're delirious! You'll never
get back. How in hell do you expect to get
back—across the sand and the sea and the cities
and the farms and the mountains and the plains and
the empty, barren swamps—back? Jesus, it will take a
lot of crawling, even using her smile to find your
way in the dark. And what if you do get
back, what then? You can't make adjustments just by ringing
a doorbell. There will be moods. There will be attitudes.
There will be words spoken and words left unsaid. It
will be a peacetime war that will go on and
on and on and you will never really get it
out of you. People will see you behaving normally and
they will remark about how well you have managed to

fit yourself back into the community, and they will congratulate
your wife on her understanding helpfulness. But you have lived
in each other's mailboxes too long and she has conditioned
herself to your absence, and you, in turn, have found
her physical presence not entirely indispensable. And so there will
be a little block of strangeness that will have to
be chipped and sculpted before you are able to recognize
once again the girl who had walked in your sleep.

It is a good thing that the human mind can
function like a digestive organ and eliminate what it chooses
to forget and let its diseased droppings harden and gather
dust in some hidden drainage ditch, and out of revulsion
idealize neat, antiseptic thinking. But there should always be someone
to sit in judgment over your application to forget and
stamp it with approval, because only those qualified to forget
should be permitted to do so. All others should remember
and should be periodically reminded that when the world owed
them a living they sent somebody else to collect it.

Life is a magnificent purse of gold thrown in people's
laps, and all they have brains enough to hold onto
is a bent penny. Peace is an interval created by
killing those who disagree, and God is notified to take
out citizenship papers or be deported. They memorialize the ruins
of faith while hope for the simple humanity of humans
is corroded in salt water—sweat, tears and the sea.

People don't know how to live. They only have suspicions.

59

When there was only one man in the world there
were problems, and when there were two men in the
world there were twice as many problems, and when another
man came along the problems were multiplied by three. But
now there are many more men and there are many
more problems and they've reproduced and spread themselves all over
the earth in a great, crawling germ. Wherever you go
you find men and their problems and they are built
one on top of the other in an opulent, spongy
congealment that asphyxiates the mind in a tangled anarchy of
ideas. It is a jungle of the spirit, and there
are trails that lead nowhere and the chunky, unshepherded growth
flowers into a sickly phantasm. And just as there are
scientific names for grasses and shrubs and vines and ferns
and trees, so too there are labels for these equivalent
flora, like Planning and Power and Competitive Systems and Centralization
and Interdependence and Liberals and Conservatives and Reactionaries and
                    Radicals
and Standards of Living and Economic Control and Security and
Resources and Geography and Profit and Classes and National Honor.
It's a cumulative canker that keeps on adding to itself
in a frenzied orgasm of incarnation, and you'd have to
deduct one man from another all the way back to
the first man before you could discover what it means.

The mind came before words and the mind came before
ideas and the mind was the pursuer and not the
pursued. But now it's a turnabout chase and the mind
is the harried quarry and it cringes and is afraid.
Living is an empty pot and thinking is a can-opener
hanging from a pantry shelf and all the ingredients that
you mix into your life are taken from classified tins
with printed directions. You cannot improvise a recipe or escape
from the formula or deviate from accepted preparations. And it
is only when circumstance has swept the cupboard bare that

you learn the pudding's proof is not how a man
has spent his life but how he has ended it.

You are striving to recall a pattern. Surely, you know
how to die. Your father did it and his father
did it and so did his and his. There must
be something inside of you that will tell you what
procedure to follow, what last gesture you must make, what
music of the muscles, design of nerve and movement and
reflex. Listen for a cue. It will come. And your
whole face will light up with knowledge. Yes, you will
know how it is done, and you will do it
directly and unhesitatingly, just as it was done before you.

This is the animated earth that goes busily among stars.
Grass in the breeze. Breeze tugging at leaves. Leaves falling
in mud. Mud sustaining grass. All this in six days
with rest on the seventh. It's been a short week.

Well, you have eaten of its food and you have
drunk its water and you have warmed yourself by its
heat. You have walked on its surface, you have dug
into its being, you have felt of it when you
had need of strength. It has sheltered you from danger and
it has hidden you from the sight of your enemies
and taken you to its breast and given you a
couch to lie upon in your large exhaustion. And now
it asks you to repay the debt, and you can
do no more than give back what you have taken.

So toss the world over your shoulder for good luck.

60

Home is the hunter, home from the hill, and all
that you have hunted you bring in your arms, and
all that you bring is nothing. It is languorously quiet
and you feel enervated into the future and thought is
a burden you would like to put down somewhere and
run away from. Solitude is the only thing you are
conscious of and you are surprised that loneliness can become
a presence. It's like seeing a hand outstretched and grasping
it and unaccountably finding that it is your own. And
in the intimacy of self encountering self at long last,
all other awarenesses withdraw as though they had tactlessly intruded.

Advance, friend. Advance and be recognized. Salute and pass on
and take your place in ranks in a position of
rest. It's easy to sleep when you know you won't
have to get up again, but it's not so deep
a slumber nor so still a silence that it will
not break when your name is being called once more.

You cannot see the war because of all the fighting
and you cannot see its ugliness because of the stinking
horror and you cannot see humanity because of the people.
Everybody is born with an umbilical cord sticking out of
his navel and its purpose is not wholly the binding
of mother to son but the knotting together of man
to man. You walked through the jungle and Lindstrom and
Egan and Whitney were in front of you and you
were behind them, and between you there was connecting tissue.
It was not because of any similarity you may have
had in thought or behavior or habit or belief, but
because you had groped for it and found it and
it had drawn you close. One of you fell down
and another picked him up and carried him in the
simple compulsion of linked survival, and that is the parallel
transcending tribe and race in the utter need of existence.

There are symbols that remain unsearched and secrets that are
locked in miracles and elusive equations that cannot be solved
merely by turning to the back of the book. But
the sun is standing still and the sands are heated
and the hill is floating up to embrace you and
the trees are hoisting their shimmering green banners of hope.
And the sound of Taps ends on a high note . . .

You do not hear the continuing noise of battle from
the beach where the Jap counterattacking force is rapidly being
annihilated, or the clamor and disorder of retreat directly below
where the enemy has lost his positions and now streams
wildly back to join with reinforcements in the rear. You
do not see the bending bushes yielding to the press
of stampeding brown bodies, some transporting wounded and others cradling
machine guns and none looking back. You do not hear
the Americans shouting orders and regrouping in skirmish lines and
bringing up mortars and ammunition and calling for a medic.

You do not see the unwashed face of Private Whitney
poke itself through the grass and survey the ground in
clinical analysis, then wave to the other members of your
squad emerging from the brush. You do not see him
approach you at a crouch and look down at the
hole in your side and lift up your left wrist
and press his finger against it to detect a pulse.
You do not hear Lieutenant Nixon come forward to the
group and ask Whitney whether or not you're still alive.

"Lieutenant," he replies, "there is nothing moving but his watch."